Emma Neale was born in Dunedin but has lived in England since 1991, where she is completing her PhD on expatriate New Zealand women writers, including Mansfield, Hyde, Frame and Adcock.

She has had poetry published in various magazines and journals in the UK and New Zealand. This is her first novel.

For Ruth

night swimming

Emma Neale

Emma Neale

London 1999

VINTAGE

With thanks and acknowledgement to Chris and Barbara Else of TFS
Literary Agency, for their patience, support and enthusiasm;
to Jane Parkin, for editing; to Bill Manhire, for past advice;
to Brian Phillips, Jane Connor and Sarah Bowden.
With special thanks to Phyllis Richardson, USA/UK,
and with thanks and love to Danny Baillie.

Vintage New Zealand
Random House New Zealand Limited
(An imprint of the Random House Group)

18 Poland Road, Glenfield,
Auckland 10, New Zealand

Sydney   New York   Toronto
London   Auckland   Johannesburg
and agencies throughout the world

First published 1998

© Emma Neale 1998
The moral rights of the Author have been asserted

ISBN 1 86941 376 8

Printed in Malaysia

All rights reserved. No part of this publication may be reproduced or
transmitted in any form or by any means, electronic or mechanical,
including photocopying, recording, storage in any information retrieval
system or otherwise, without the written permission of the publisher.

For Danny
For Jim
For Barbara
For Sarah

I think I saw Jenny today. A hemisphere away and fifteen years later. It may have been a mistake, I suppose—a false assumption. Yet that implies I have casually, naturally assumed, and how could I possibly expect her? How unlikely it is. Why would my mind finally join her name with a stranger's face, here in London, as neatly and fittingly as the last two letters in a crossword clue?

I try to reason with myself—impossible that it was her.

In our New Zealand town, and then right across the country, there was no trace of her for so many months that her case was simply 'left open', as the police detective interviewed on television said, worn and ashen after working weeks of overtime, days and nights undivided. I remember his hand passing over his face as he turned away from the camera. He was the father of another girl in our year.

'Jenny, Jenny, Jenny Wren', I used to sing out from the gate when I came by to pick her up on the way to school. Her eyes green, like thin chips of bottle glass held to the light, her head movements quick, her laugh a scale of notes that could suddenly crack a silence and have everyone limp with giggles. It was this laugh that I thought I recognised first today. Above the intermittent dry rustle of morning newspapers and occasional, muted conversation, the notes gave out across the train carriage. I looked up with such a start that several people near me also looked in the direction I sought, before they lowered their heads back to their papers, gentle and slow as cattle. The laugh repeated, half familiar, a coded signal. I stood up, hardly knowing what instinct made me do so. I had a tingling sensation in my chest and throat; a light, celebrational balloon was filling and rising in my body. And then, close by, yet separated from me by several passengers in the rush-hour crush, I saw her.

Her head was tipped towards her companion. Her hair was Jenny's natural colour—perhaps an odd thing for me to notice: it had the sheen and reddish tint of a ripe, tight-skinned horse chestnut just freed from its spiny green pod. Her brothers had always teased her about it, called her Gingernut. I knew that when the sun hit single strands, sometimes you could see a metallic red, bold as tinsel, at others the white of drought-dried grass. The woman I was watching was fairly tall, and dressed in a belted outfit that dropped to her ankles in a full skirt, like the mouth of a bell. Light cinnamon freckles sprinkled her face, which otherwise was pale—although her cheeks were healthily round when she smiled.

Taking in these details, there were still small differences that made me hesitant. I stared hard, unnoticed by her. Lines on each side of her mouth had appeared, as had sets near her eyes, like a child's sketch of cat whiskers. More lines travelled across her forehead, and as her expression grew serious the angles of her profile seemed more—emphatic—than I remembered. It was as if determination had worked a steady current over her face, shaping and reshaping it over time. I recalled a school play season, when I had done the make-up for the cast backstage and had been asked to age Jenny, following the natural lines of her face. Now I felt the pulse in my throat strengthen.

I strained to hear the woman speak, as our train hurtled in the darkness between stations, buffeting and bumping. She shifted her balance every now and then, fluidly, gracefully, while other travellers—those with small towers of luggage anxiously labelled with their destinations—lurched and made startled lunges at poles. I tried to attune my ear to the woman's voice. The accent seemed neutral at first, unplaceable, but now and then a vowel would loosen, like a bubble of oxygen scudding up to the water's surface. I leaned in as a piano tuner might, wanting her to go over and over her 'i's. I became sure I could detect an antipodean pronunciation; the familiar intonations were just shimmering in the short runs of her speech.

The train's speed began to slacken. I tried to squeeze my way through the spaces left by a small cluster of businesswomen in candy-coloured, short-skirted suits. The woman I thought was Jenny had begun to move towards the automatic double doors. One of the executives, her hair powerfully scented with lacquer, exaggerated the inconvenience I was causing, giving a laboured swing to one side as if I had elbowed her. I murmured to appease her, and the woman—Jenny—readied her shoulder bag as she reached the doors for her exit from the train. Desperation to get to her finally flooded me completely, and I pushed harder through the narrow gap. The train stopped and the doors slid apart. The woman stepped towards the opening.

'Jenny!' I said. People near the door must have sensed my panic: they stood back now, or turned sideways to let me past.

'Jen!' She gave a small hop down onto the platform, where her companion touched her briefly on the elbow.

'*Jenny!*'

I realise now that I should have stepped down to join them, but it was as if I needed her confirmation first, and was still slowly filling with realisation: a vessel growing heavier as water is poured into it, the shock not delayed, but delaying.

She turned, surprised, and looked straight at me as I stood in the doorway. Her face was expectant, puzzled, but then impersonal—and blank. No. Of course—Jenny had never held herself quite like that. My hand dropped to my side—I realised I'd been holding it out to her, asking her to grasp my arms so that I could pull her back onto the train.

The curved glass doors began to close. I felt embarrassment leak into my face, a hot wine stain. The train gave a jerk as the driver released the brakes. Then, through the carriage window, I saw the woman's expression change. Her eyes widened, her lips parted, and, as the platform seemed to move independently backwards, I seized the last images. I saw her body flinch upright at a sharp, inward punch of air. One hand went to her chest, and then slowly, gently, something in her expression softened and lifted as the train hummed and pulled away.

Hours later, after work, and when Joss had come home, I was still shaken. I had been late for my shift: had left my train at the next stop and journeyed backwards to the station where I had seen Jenny, expecting that if it had been her she would have stayed, hoping I'd return . . .

I searched for her by the ticket booths, then up and down the platforms. When I couldn't find her, I began to puzzle over and over the scene, my mind crossing and recrossing her expression, like a tracker dog trying to find one girl's trail in a school playground. Was it her? Did she recognise me? I had nothing as evidence that the scene had even happened: no slip of paper with her address and number; no entry in my diary of a time and place to meet; not even a strand of her hair or a plum-coloured thread from the hem of her skirt that had brushed from her coat onto mine, as a talisman. Nothing physical to reassure me that my mind hadn't just been projecting elaborate, seductive holograms.

Although I had been half an hour late that morning, Doctor Kershaw let me leave the surgery early. I help out with his admin for a ridiculously fast-paced fifteen hours a week: the job is helping to put me through my postgrad diploma in social work.

Doctor Kershaw clocked me over the rims of his glasses as he brought me a set of patients' records. The files were liberally polkadotted with rings of red where he'd highlighted mistakes. I realised that the angle of my chin and my clasped hands, which had unconsciously begun to crumple the proof-read pages, must have seemed beseeching as his eyes focused on mine, intense as an examination torch.

'Not well?' he asked.

My typing was usually pristine. The mistakes needed an explanation.

'No, I'm fine. It's just—I've had some—difficult news today.'

Doctor Kershaw nodded, checked his watch and said something about a committee meeting. He rested a hand on my computer as if it were a shoulder.

'I suppose we can spare you after five,' he said, and gave the machine a brisk series of pats. 'Give you time to absorb this—ah—news.' He waited, perhaps expecting a shared confidence now that he had been warmly avuncular. A sudden picture of Jenny's head tipped back in laughter came to me. I nodded, and called up a patient's file on screen, scrutinising the text in the hope that both Doctor Kershaw and the ache of that vivid snapshot would leave me.

Since then, I've been alone with my thoughts, so absorbed that I barely recall the journey home, or what I've done at the flat between the hours of six and eight, although my study notes are spread before me when Joss's key scrabbles in the lock. His arrival is like a sudden shift in time zones. I have to force myself to refocus: my mind has shuttered into its own deep silence, like a covered lens.

Joss dumps his coat, goes to the hall table to check for mail, one hand pulling off his tie.

'All right?' he asks, a distracted non-question. I 'hmmm' and go off to the kitchen to pour us a beer: a pause while we expand into a mood for genuine conversation.

When he comes into the kitchen, I begin to shift plates and glasses around aimlessly from surface to surface. Then I offer him a glass of beer, and the hand that holds it towards him is like an animal entirely separate from myself. The skin white and drawn tightly to the bones, it trembles, a thin dog kicked in the ribs. Joss reaches out and cups his palm over my knuckles.

'Are you cold?' he asks. I shake my head. A dark mark appears between his eyebrows: a small trench formed by his frown whenever he's worried. When we first met, I would sometimes wet my thumb and try to wipe away what I thought was an inky smudge on his brow, only to feel the tiny muscles bunched there. Sometimes a minute nerve kicked away under my touch as if irritably pushing me away. I've never liked causing these signs of tension in him, so I sit down at the kitchen table, smiling briefly, and pull out another chair.

He takes his glass in one hand, still holding my hand with the other as he swirls his beer, watching the small head coat the top of the rim.

Nearly nine years ago now, and more than a year after we first met, I told him about Jenny for the first time. We were sitting on a couch at a party, drinking, and I knew even then the conversation was incongruous, anti-social. There we were, an acknowledged couple; we could talk to each other any time we wanted. We should have been circulating to help out our hosts, friends with whom Joss taught at an inner-city school.

I was aware of more and more people arriving, some smiling and moving over to our side of the room. Their faces were bright, the light rain from outside glistening on their skins and clinging like a net of fine glass beads to the dark hair of one of the men. Yet somehow Joss and I had started on a subject we couldn't abandon. We were sitting side by side on a lumpy, second-hand sofa, its arms nearly at the point of collapse: between the cushions were old cigarette packets, a clothes peg, a receipt, a couple of copper coins. It wasn't a setting private enough for what I was trying to explain, yet I found myself talking with an accuracy that had always eluded me. Joss watched me in silence. I finished with emotion compressed into my throat like an acrid capsule that wouldn't go down. I thought, If he doesn't speak, or do something, I will have to get up and walk out of the room.

Joss took my plastic cup, put it on the floor and gripped my hand so tightly that I had to flex my fingers apart when he finally let go.

'Sometimes, I still think Jenny could be alive,' I said to him, after telling him what had happened when I was seventeen. 'I want her to still be alive. And I could accept that she'd betrayed me. I could.'

We haven't spoken of those events recently—perhaps not for years. I even wonder if he remembers what I told him. Like many of the confessions we made during our early years together, it has gone underground, buried with a quiet mutual consent. So many secrets: a kind of terrible treasure.

I squeeze his hand. Suddenly, in our cool and slightly damp kitchen, the fear and panic from Jenny's disappearance all those years ago come back as more than a memory—it all comes back living, flares along my blood. A question leaps from me.

'Where do I have scars?'

Joss looks a little exasperated, sits back in his chair and scratches at his scalp with both hands while he stretches out his back. I hear the small click of his spine realigning.

'What do you mean?' He takes a swig of beer, leaving a thin stripe of froth on his upper lip. I run my finger along his mouth and give it to him to taste.

'Just that—where do I have scars? Do you remember? And do you remember where I have birthmarks?'

He squints at me. 'Well, you've got a birthmark—somewhere—and then there's, well, obviously, there's your appendix scar . . .'

I remember the description released by the police of Jenny's clothing—the outfit her father thought she was probably wearing when she left the house the last time he saw her. The vagueness of it: the way the items and colours blurred into each other, hazed over, seemed to question one another. 'A dark or navy-blue sweatshirt or jumper. Blue denim jeans or cotton trousers, faded. Tennis shoes, light or sky blue with white . . .' As if Jenny were already becoming less distinct in people's minds. Was already fading.

'Do you remember what I was wearing this morning?'

Joss's eyes travel my body and he smiles. 'What are you getting at?'

I know I'm being obtuse, but these questions are too important for explanations. What warning is there when someone just vanishes?

'Do you?'

He shrugs. 'Black trousers, forest-green shirt, black jacket?' Exactly what he sees in front of him.

I take a sip of my beer, swallow, and slowly shake my head. 'I've changed,' I say. 'I spilt coffee on the dress I was wearing when you left this morning.'

'Look, Marie. Is something important going on here? Why are you asking me all this?'

Jenny, Jenny, of the bright brown hair. Jenny my friend. Do you remember the first time we met?

Walking out of the school gates, aged fourteen, third week of the term. We crossed to the same side of the road, and headed in the same direction. Jenny drew alongside me with all the confidence of someone completely at ease in her territory, barely checking over her shoulder for cars as she loped across the second lane. I waited for her to pass. I was new to the school, and had realised that my classmates were locked fast into friendships that had formed the year before.

'Hiya,' she said, cracking at a thick, white wad of gum. I

could smell its artificial fragrance. 'I've seen you before,' she said, 'walking to school.'

'Oh?' I didn't like thinking I'd been watched. Next to what I could instantly see was Jenny's easy grace, everything about me could be the butt of ridicule. I looked askance at her walking beside me: her narrow waist, the crisp white blouse, her school uniform skirt taken up far higher than my mother would have allowed. Mine hung below my knees—'because you'll grow, and starting in about ten seconds,' my mother had said.

Jenny saw that I was looking at her skirt. She openly measured the length of mine, and raised her eyes. 'Your face stands out in a crowd,' she said.

'What?' I expected some kind of piquant sarcasm next, some comment about my jutting chin, the large forehead that my mother and sisters always tried to get me to disguise with a looser hairdo. ('Why do you scrape your hair back so? You've just got no idea, have you?') I had an immediate image of myself in a crowd of blue uniforms, my big pasty face looming above everyone like a street lamp, my teeth protruding out like a chalky overhanging cliff as I laughed.

I fired a look at Jenny, but she gave a casual shrug. 'It just stands out. I've noticed you.'

She held out some gum. 'Like some?' I shook my head. She looked quizzically at the packet, then spat out the fat, sticky wedge her jaws had been working at, and flicked it into a rubbish bin left out for street collection. 'Gives me a headache after a while. Only chewed it to see how many classes I could get through without it being confiscated. Confiscated! Like taking stuff covered in someone else's saliva is *such* a strong act of authority. *Right.*'

I felt my heart do a somersault of recognition and admiration, as if she'd talked back, on my behalf, in a situation where I would never have dared. I laughed. 'Yeah, I reckon most of them are just jealous 'cause they can't chew chutty with their false teeth.'

Jenny grinned.

We'd already reached the end of the main road, where I had to turn off. I tried to think of how to prolong our conversation. Jenny stood, legs slightly apart, her hands plunged into her blazer pockets, elbows out, a broad smile on her face. She reminded me, strangely, of black and white photos in my grandmother's albums of men with caps pushed to the back of their heads, shirt sleeves rolled up, standing proudly next to freshly built houses in a landscape scabbed from pioneer fires.

'Coming to my place?' she asked.

Later, I realised her posture was learned from her brothers: her silent allies. At the time, I put my hands in my own blazer pockets, and half-consciously copied her straddle-legged stance, trying both to look casual and to hide my elation.

'Sure,' I said.

She laughed, as if she'd guessed all along that I'd say yes, and she spun on her heel.

I can remember her style so clearly; the way she moved was as distinctive as if sealed into her with the complexity and detail of a fingerprint. I would even be able to distinguish her favourite clothes, the ones she wore all those years ago, if they were retrieved for an exhibit, for evidence. There was the light blue, Indian cotton skirt that she loved: it fell in crinkles and was sewn with vertical lines of thin silver thread. The waistband tassels had small silver bells tied to the ends—Jenny would always silence them in a clutched hand whenever she wanted to pass through the house without her stepmother knowing her movements.

I knew her like a lover. Better than a lover: for as we went through the last four years of school, we formed ourselves together. Tried to make ourselves in another image: the image of what we wanted to be. Teachers began to confuse which of us was which, not because our physical appearances were at all alike, but because we were inseparable. We were a double-barrelled entity: JennyandMarie. And we were loaded, high-cocked to go off in a blaze of hope. Hope is what we'd have called it then, I suppose. Now I think it was youth. An eaten fuse.

Joss runs a finger down the bridge of my nose. I catch his hand and push it away.

'Describe me.'

'Tell me what's got into you, first.'

'What if you had to do it one day? Describe me.'

He leans in as if trying to detect a scent. 'Have you been drinking without me?'

'*No.*' I thump my glass onto the table, harder than I mean to. A small wave of beer slops over my wrist and runs to the floor. 'Joss, please. It's important.'

And I see something in him relent. Something tender.

There in the kitchen he runs his hands over my head, then my hair, lifts it from the nape of my neck. He describes what he touches. I unbutton my blouse, stand, and turn as he traces my skin. He fingers moles on my back, smoothes the small café au lait birthmark that is splashed over my ribs like an accidental spillage of ink. When he reaches my waist, I unbuckle my trousers and he touches the pink appendix scar as if silencing a mouth. He tells me of the two dark hollows at the base of my spine, above my buttocks; finds the speckling of lavender and red on one knee—a childhood scar from being pushed over in a playground line for Four Square. Tiny pieces of gravel had pierced and lodged in the skin. At home my mother had sterilised her tweezers in boiling water, and I heard the tips grate as they tried to grip the chips of asphalt. Joss runs his hand down my shins, and reaches my feet, where the small toe on my right foot is bent awkwardly outwards, like the claw of a hermit crab feeling its way across the sand. He rubs it between his thumb and index finger as if relieving pain.

Joss rises from where he has bent to my feet, and slips a hand underneath the cup of my bra. He leans in to kiss me, but I take a step back. 'Again,' I say. 'Memorise me.'

He waits there, as still as a man listening for footsteps. But he begins his trail again, narrating in a low, slow voice.

Then he unbuttons his own shirt, watching me fixedly. I go over his body, under my breath, running his skin beneath my hands like prayer beads, to an internal chart I've already memorised. There is a scooped out coin of flesh over one vertebra in his neck, where he scraped it once, falling on a sharp concrete step. There is stitching over one eyebrow—as pale as nylon fishing line, so slender and faint it is barely visible. He can't remember how it happened. There is a bolder scar running down his calf, alongside the length of his shinbone, but he can remember that, as do I. I drove with him in the cab to the hospital. He had opened his calf muscle like a pea pod with a knife when he'd slipped and driven his cleated track shoe into one leg during a race meet. Lying on the Astroturf, he told me later, he thought he'd seen the silky underside of the muscle, creamy and soft as the inner coating of a fresh green bean—but he had tried to stand, as if the image in his sightline hadn't fully transmitted to his shocked brain. The white split had filled with blood as soon as he stood, and the leg crumpled beneath him. The doctor at the hospital used a hooked needle and blue thread the colour of veins seen through skin. She neatly sutured the lips of the wound, as practical as someone mending the hem of a skirt. Joss limped out, the garment of his fit body tucked and altered, and his calf already invisibly repairing, making what would be the angry, criss-crossed stripes of scar tissue. It has faded only slightly over the past year or so.

As I reach this scar, Joss begins to shiver in the chill of the unheated kitchen. He holds me to him briefly for warmth, and then quietly pulls away, watching my face, assessing me. After a moment, in answer to his own implied question, he gathers up our clothes. Shivering again, we clamber back into them as if we've just towelled ourselves dry following a plunge into a wintry sea.

Joss digs a box of matches out from one of his pockets and goes to light a gas element. He stands with his hands hovering over the flames.

'Are you going to tell me what's happened?' he asks.

I couldn't bear to be humoured over this. I hope he feels a twinge of fear—that he fears what would happen if I were lost.

Apart from the rush and bubble of the gas, the silence between us fills the room, cool, blue and still. Then I throw my stone, skimming and skipping over the surface.

'I think I saw Jenny today.'

How unformed I was, before I met Jenny. How she altered me. Yet as I recall it all, I'm gradually overtaken by those adolescent feelings again. As I start to explain to Joss, I can hear that girl in my voice. I ought to shake myself, remind myself how much time has passed since then, how much else I have done and seen, but the events from those years lift and carry me along with them as if I'm as light as the foam on a storm-swollen stream.

The year before I met Jen, my family nickname was the Worrywort. I could get nervous about just about anything. Even walking home from school—although *that* had a lot to do with boys. They confused me. It was the seniors from the local boys' secondary school before we moved who had this effect on me. Twice a week members of the First Fifteen walked the same route that I did. I was afraid of their loud confidence and their movement in a pack; I was always alone, and they would deliberately take up the breadth of the footpath as they approached me. If I swung out onto the road to avoid them, there was always one who would make contact—an elbow brushing mine, a shoulder knocking against my shoulder like a glancing billiard ball, the deep, emphatic 'So - rry!' They'd all stand aside to watch me, scattering like birds that seemed to know the next position in a flight pattern, magpies in their black blazers and white shirts, anticipating some flash of silver. Jenny just managed to laugh at things like that. 'Get some *specs*; look where you're going, Dorkbreath!' she'd fling over her shoulder. Then to me she'd mutter, 'And get some acne cream while he's at it. His face makes me want to chunder.'

Jenny was a godsend, my mother thought. At least at first.

Mum worried about me and boys. But not quite the way other mothers did. She wanted my sisters and I coupled off, wanted us to attract the 'right kind': men who wouldn't hurt us, who'd fit into the picture of happiness she'd formed after my father had been her own rescue. She lived a second youth through us, loving the coming and going, the whirling and laughing of my older sisters. 'Have a *wonderful* time!' she would call out to them, as if each outing were some exotic holiday, after which they'd unzip their cases of souvenirs and she'd marvel and revel in the details.

'Oh, what I'd have given to have had your chances!' she would say: a reference to her own father's strictness. My grandfather had apparently let my uncles 'get away with murder' (they swore, drank and settled arguments with their fists), but he had insisted on escorting my mother to and from all social occasions. Any keen beau who tried to accompany her had to put up with my grandfather's rigid silence between them. I imagined him: stiff, hard-bitten, glinting like a sword placed for chastity between them, and each poor boy coming away nicked and bleeding, jawbone dotted with little spots of tissue paper.

Before I knew Jenny, my mother was always urging me to take up badminton, or join worthy causes that would get me to 'meet people'—though what she meant was meet boys. She worried that I was too solitary and too brooding. She'd tap on my door at the weekend, when I was reading or listening to the radio, and she'd say, her voice mounting with delight, 'It's a *lovely* day, Marie. Lucy and Heather are off to watch the local cricket—why don't you go along?'

I didn't want to be like Heather and Lucy. Pink, frothy and stupid. If my mother hadn't let me see her—even mild—disappointment, I might not have resisted her so resolutely. But I'd say, 'I'd love to, Mum, it's just that I've got a social studies project due next week, and it's really difficult . . .'

Her face would try so hard not to show discouragement, but she couldn't win against schoolwork.

'This school seems to give you so much more study than Lucy and Heather ever had, dear.'

'But I need to work hard. To make sure I get anywhere.'

This was my lowest possible blow. Both my sisters were re-sitting School Certificate, Heather for the third and Lucy for the second time, and neither of them could see the point in school. On my own first day at high school my form teacher had read out the roll and said, 'Marie Conway? You're not related to Heather and Lucy are you?' She pointed at me with her folder. 'Are you another dizzy little flibbertigibbet?' I was humiliated. And galvanised. I'd show them.

As I laboured away at my schoolwork over those weekends before I knew Jen, my father would sometimes tap on my door as well, saying he was driving my sisters to their netball matches, or their hockey tournaments, and would I like to go along? Dressed in a tracksuit and sports shoes, though he was going only to stand on the sidelines, he'd pop his head round my doorway, his face already ruddy with satisfaction. He had a look of repletion that said, 'My eldest—they're good sports. Solid team members . . . it's not about winning, is it? You've got to have your hobbies, don't you?'

I'd wave my looseleaf paper at him, with what I hoped was an absorbed frown, and he'd make a characteristic noise of his, sucking at his back teeth.

'Books, books, books, eh? All work and no play? Well, you

know we'd love to have you along.' And although that gave me a pang of gratitude, I'd shake my head. 'Ah, well,' Dad would sigh a little, 'they can't say you didn't get my brains!' Then he'd wink, and leave, to bounce gently on his heels in the driveway until Heather and Lucy appeared with their sportsbags.

My sisters were only a year apart: Heather three and Lucy four years older than I. They had always been close: so close that sometimes I thought of them, Mum and Dad as a separate family, one that existed alongside Mum, Dad and me. Perhaps the perception springs from a memory of one hot afternoon, when Lucy and Heather cartwheeled backwards and forwards through the sprinkler jets on the lawn while I watched from the doorstep, biding my time before I edged over to them, holding up my hands to catch the falling water. As I entered the spray, they lost interest in their game and ran inside. Dad, watching, put aside his spade, then stepped under the sprinkler in all his gardening clothes. As he reached out his hand, mine crept over my stomach. I went to the garden tap and turned off the water. Then there was a quietness. Dripping, Dad's arms reached down, and he picked me up. I didn't mind the coolness of his wet shirt. I rested my hot cheek against the damp, and asked him to sing the song with the chorus, 'So they all rolled over and one fell out . . .' He whispered it under his breath as he carried me inside, squeezing me closer to him each time he reached the line, 'And the little one said, "roll over, roll over!"'

My refusal to go to my sister's sports matches came not only from a deliberate wish to maintain my distance from them. I disliked family outings in general: all those obligatory picnics, afternoon teas and dinners with my aunts and uncles, which became monotonously regular soon after our shift.

On one of these occasions I disgraced myself by making Heather cry. She had been ordering me around, telling me to move this, lift that, lay out the picnic rug and make sure it was all straight . . . I hadn't wanted to go along in the first place, so told her she was a big fat bossy bitch, and in that yellow hand-me-down sundress looked just like a giant grapefruit: wasn't it funny that she'd ended up with the same battleship hips as Auntie Julie? Heather sobbed, Auntie Julie overheard, and my father commanded me to go and *sit* in the car. It simply confirmed my conviction that *nobody ever even asked me anything about what I wanted*. After that, I resolutely refused any family occasions I could. I had to prove I didn't have to do things their way.

Yet when we were little, I'd often had a sense that the way I did things was wrong. My sisters always hushed up what they said when I came near, or they ran away too quickly for me to catch up. They pretended to be twins sometimes, and I don't remember them ever having the same bitter fights with each other that they had with me. By the time I was fourteen, and came to meet Jenny, my sisters and I were learning how to orbit each other more widely, and I began to see less of them. I liked it better that way.

My mother loved Heather's and Lucy's breezy busyness, but worried about them not applying themselves at school; and she loved me as her little one, the one she least wanted to let go. But I was also a puzzle to her.

Once, I must have been about ten, I heard my mother telling one of her friends in the kitchen, over their coffee cups, that I was 'an odd little thing'. That for some time she had worried about me but was coming to accept that I wasn't as gregarious as my sisters. 'She's so solitary. She plays perfectly well with the other kids at school, the teachers say, but there's no one special—do you know what I mean? She never brings a little friend home.' Her own friend had murmured, the spoon stirring in the thick ceramic mug, making a 'tsk, tsk' sound as it knocked against the sides.

I remember being frozen in the hallway, shame and anger flushing through me. My mother was talking about me 'behind my back', as I'd heard the kids at school accuse one another of doing. And I did feel something at my back, as if an ice cube scuttled down my spine. Something had been confirmed, or a hidden picture had been released from a page—like the colouring books I had, which only needed a brush dipped in water to make several shades blossom on the paper's skin, filling in the simple outlines. All along, there'd been this secret about me that I hadn't known. I looked 'solitary' up in the dictionary. *On my own*. It became something I expected of myself, and so I never really tried to change it. Until I met Jen.

'Why can't you girls be less extreme?' Mum asked, years later, in a particularly exasperated version of our weekend ritual. She hit the tea-tray she was carrying against her thigh. '*You* should get *out*, and they should stay *in*! And I wish you wouldn't set yourself such high expectations, Marie.' She smoothed a hand over my hair. 'I don't like to see you so worried. Balance is best, don't you think? Why don't you tag along with Heather and Lucy? You might meet someone.'

I should have just laughed, but I tossed my pen onto my desk in annoyance. Why didn't my parents ever praise me? Say, 'Marie, you've worked so hard!'? It felt like they were always trimming me back, even overlooking me because my sisters had done things first. They were the normality against which I'd always be measured.

'*Mum*,' I answered, 'Heather and Lucy have more than enough social life for all three of us.'

She opened her arms as if catching a bouquet, then clapped them together again, trying to tease me. 'Oh Marie, Marie,' she sang, 'you're jealous!'

All these efforts by my mother to make me *socialise*, to make me *popular*, to meet *boys*, had succeeded only in making me oversensitive and jittery in certain situations. Which was why, when I entered Jenny's house on that very first afternoon, I felt a tightening screw of nerves in my stomach. I suspected she had brothers even before I saw them. Past the threshold of her front door there was a presence unlike that of my own house, in which memories of the previous owners still lingered, and which now was so dominated by women.

In Jenny's corridor there was a row of grubby oilskins as we came in, the hoods hanging off a series of hooks. There was a smell that made me think of boat yards: ropey, salty, mixed with tarpaulin and a faint lacing of diesel. The empty shapes suspended there already suggested the weight and height of adolescent boys. As we passed the bathroom, the door of which was propped open, a large, dark form dangling from the shower rail made me jump. Jenny gave her lifting laugh. 'It's okay, it's not a body. It's Jonathon's scuba suit.' The sleeves and leggings were full and slightly angled at the knees and elbows, shaped to fit snugly to someone's limbs. Water trickled from the cuffs into the bath, as if the thing had just surfaced from its habitual murky underworld.

I could hear the sound of a radio and someone clinking together dishes in the kitchen. A black dog padded out into the hallway, and Jenny bent to give it a quick hug. It wandered off again, a caretaker doing its rounds. As we made our way to the back of the house, passing various rooms, I expected a shadowy shape to glide to one of the doorways, somehow disembodied like the coats and scuba suit: a male form that hovered, the reverse of a torchlight, looming and immense, and suddenly enfolding me in its cool, deep echo, like the mouth of a cave. I wanted to go home—wished I hadn't agreed so quickly to Jenny's spontaneous invitation.

'I'll see if you can stay for dinner,' Jenny said. 'I'll ask Marion.'
'Marion?'
'My step-mum.'

She led me into the kitchen, while I tried to think up a reason for having to be home and braced myself for an encounter with the inhabitants of the oilskins.

One of her brothers, Jonathon, was sitting on a kitchen stool, leafing through a magazine on motocross racing. Unlike Jenny, he was blond, but like her, freckled. He glanced up, said 'Hi', then slid off his stool. He hadn't met my eye—but then I was nervously glancing from Jenny to him as if caught between two lanes of fast traffic.

'Is Marion home?' Jenny asked.

'Yep,' he answered. He slid the magazine off the bench, rolled it into a baton and gently thwacked the top of Jenny's head. Then he turned to me, as if all the time he'd been monitoring me in his peripheral vision.

'Hi,' he said again. It was a question. I nodded.

'This is Marie,' Jenny grinned at me. 'She's staying for dinner. Is Gareth around?'

'Nahp. He's probably staying at Mark's.' Jonathon looked at me again, openly curious. 'You a mute?'

I shook my head, which made him laugh.

'So say something.'

He leaned an elbow on the kitchen bench with a laziness that matched his voice and said he was readying himself for teasing combat. Jenny was watching me too, with a slightly tense curiosity. I could see the golden hairs of Jonathon's thighs, where his grey woollen school shorts ended. Even relaxed, with most of his weight supported by the bench, his quad muscles were pronounced, squared. Although I paid him enough attention to notice these details, the way he eyed me made me want to inspect my clothes.

'I'm not sure I can stay for dinner,' I said, and pulled my blazer over my breasts. They felt sensitised, as if the lashes of Jonathon's eyes had tickled over my skin.

'Don't let Jonathon put you off,' said Jenny. 'He's a dickhead.'

He shot out his impromptu baton and swiped her, sharply this time, on the arm. Just then the kitchen door bumped open, and a woman—Marion—clacked in on high, white heels as precarious as cheese sticks. I thought they looked as if they could snap, scattering crumbs, any minute.

She was short, with long permed hair that she'd tried to dye blonde but that had gone an odd, off-orange colour. Her tight, knee-length, olivey-green skirt was made of a stretch cotton material, the hem of which kept rolling up slightly, and she wore low-denier black tights, which were blotchy, as if the skin underneath were bruised. She had painful-looking scabs at the sides of her mouth, the kind small children get from persistently licking chapped lips. She'd tried to cover them with make-up; and as I took this in, and imagined how it must have stung, I was also struck by her age. How *cool* to have such a young stepmum! I glanced at Jenny, appraisingly. Where she and Jonathon had been poised for a play scuffle, their postures had changed, their faces set with a diffidence that made them look strikingly similar. Jonathon rested a hand on Jenny's shoulder, then sloped off to the door.

'Nice to meet you, Marie,' he said mildy, his eyebrows raised in a signal that struck me as oddly conspiratorial after his initial goading.

Jenny gave a smooth glide to the sink, began running water, slipped on some gloves and shifted dishes.

'This is Marie, Mum,' she said, her back turned to me and her stepmother. I noticed the shift she'd made from Marion to 'Mum': it sounded unnatural, thin and tight, like the rind around an unripe lemon. 'I've asked her to stay for dinner, so we can cook if you like.'

'Oh Jenny, look, I'm sorry. I don't have the energy tonight. I helped out at your father's office today, and I'm exhausted. Another night, perhaps.' Marion gave a quickly manufactured and quickly discarded smile.

Jenny stayed at the sink. 'Gareth's not in for dinner,' she said. 'And Marie and I have an English project to do for homework—we've been assigned together.' We weren't even in the same class, but I thought it best to nod.

Marion crossed her arms and her stare willed Jenny to turn around. Jenny carried on with the dishes, her movements slow and careful. I felt as if I were growing huge in their silence: an ugly, colourless root that they were struggling over, trying to heave me out of the stiff clods of earth between them.

'Dad wouldn't mind,' said Jenny.

'He'd mind if he knew I minded. Now don't let's argue in front of the guest, Jenny.'

Jenny plunged her hands into the water, then slammed a glass into the dish rack. 'She's hardly a guest if you're not going to let her stay, is she?'

'It's okay, really . . .' I was horribly embarrassed now, unable to figure out why Jenny had flashed out with anger but somehow feeling I should try to defuse things.

Marion's voice became shapeless and limp with fatigue, as if this was a scene they had gone through often. 'I said, let's not argue.'

Jenny shoved the rest of the dishes into the sink, then snapped off the rubber gloves, their tight sheaths cracking like small explosions. 'Someone else can do these.' She went quickly to the back door, bumped it open and ran down the steps. I didn't have much choice but to follow.

Jenny booted a stone down the footpath. 'God, she's a bitch!'

'I should go home,' I said, but I was transfixed; I'd swear she was almost green with fury. Jenny seemed equally unsure of what to do next. She stayed scuffing the pavement, and she no longer looked like the self-possessed, gum-cracking stranger of half an hour before. This emboldened me.

'I mean—wow, Jenny. I've *never* yelled at my parents for something like that. No, actually, I've never yelled at them full-stop!' I took a breath to say more, but Jenny, blinking rapidly, turned her face away. I wished immediately I hadn't said it. I'd sounded more critical than I'd meant to. But she still hovered there, waiting.

I dug the fingernails of one hand into my palm. It was a trick I had found for steeling myself to something, like walking into a new class, or past inaccessible cliques of girls, as I took myself off to the library at lunch time.

'Ummm—you can come over to my place,' I said. 'If you like.'

'Yeah?' she said. 'That'd be great.'

I unclenched my hand. Four red sickle marks smiled up from my palm, which throbbed a little. I hid my hand in my pocket, and said to Jen. It's not too far from here.

I remember that barely-being-able-to-breathe feeling as we walked up my driveway. What would she think of our new house? What on earth would we do when we got inside? I felt a stranger there myself. The house had a dry, peppery smell, and every time I went through a door I had a feeling I would stumble on someone else's belongings. I still ran my hands into the corners of desk drawers and cupboards when I opened them, hoping to find something that would link me with the house's past and explain the suffocating atmosphere the previous owners had left behind.

Jenny and I went straight to the fridge, grabbed a glass of orange cordial each, then trooped off to my room. I gestured for her to sit on the bed while I perched on my desk, feet up on a chair. I concentrated on my cordial. Any sense of what to do next trailed away.

Jenny stood up and went to the window, then came back, her eyes flicking over the room.

'That's sort of cute,' she said, pointing to a stuffed toy that I'd had since I was a toddler. I wished I'd hidden it in a cupboard.

'It's really old,' I dismissed, and looked away, scanning the room for anything else that might distract her. Everything I owned seemed suddenly tatty and childish.

I took another mouthful of drink. Acidity competed with

sugary confection. Does she like it? I thought. Or is it revolting? What does she usually have after school? I begged Jenny to think of something to say. She was still surveying the room. Finally, her gaze wandered again, to me.

'So how long have you lived here?' She sat back down on the bed.

'Just since summer.'

'Thought so. Didn't think I'd seen you at school last year. You hang out on your own a bit, don't you?'

I shrugged, and tried to sound indifferent. 'A bit.'

'So why did you move to this dump?'

For a second I thought she meant the house, and the cordial in my stomach turned.

'Did your Mum or Dad get work here or something?'

'Oh. Yeah. Dad got promoted.' I didn't add that he'd also taken the chance to move back down south to be near family, though I wished I had when she started laughing.

'To here? Promotion? We went on holiday to Australia over summer—I loved it there. It was so sunny, so busy. All the different *people*—do you know what I mean? Have you ever been overseas?'

I shook my head.

'I loved it. I'm going to travel everywhere when I leave home. You're lucky, moving around, you know. Getting to see new places. Even if it is here. What do you think of it so far?'

I didn't know how to answer. I glanced around the room as Jenny had done, then slipped off my desk and went to look out the window, into the garden. I couldn't really tell her she was the first person I'd met since we moved. And I hadn't told anyone what I thought of the new town. Not since Mum had warned me and my sisters, as we'd packed up old apple boxes with books and ornaments, how important the move was to Dad (he'd been appointed regional manager of the supermarket chain he'd worked for since leaving school) and how we had to rally together to make things go smoothly. 'We'll have to be good to him,' she'd said. 'Show we're happy for his promotion, and be supportive if he finds it tough for a while after losing Granma.'

All summer it had felt as if I were either getting in everyone's way or they weren't interested in what I wanted to do. After Dad had organised his tools, and the Civil Defence supplies which he always stored in case of earthquakes or floods, he became preoccupied and distant, working or spending time with my aunts and uncles. Moving nearer to them after my grandmother died was another reason he'd agreed to his new job. Mum in turn was taken up with work, or with him, while my sisters had adapted quickly, finding friends within a few days of our collapsing the cardboard boxes and storing them in the garden shed. When Mum briskly asked what I had done while she was at work, I'd invent things. Say I'd been to the pool or the library—when I might have walked there, then panicked, turned around and sped back again, imagining every passer-by staring and judging. Then I'd trail though the house, listless, checking the clock every half hour, unable to stop urging it on, until one day I flipped the batteries out from its back and hurled them across the room. Two small, dark bruises marked the wallpaper where they'd hit.

I'd told myself that everything would be all right once school started. But as soon as it did the summer of solitude seemed to emanate from me like a deflective shield. Once I edged in on a group of girls from my form room, and asked if I could eat lunch with them; they slid over on the wooden bleachers outside the assembly hall but carried on talking without an interruption. I started to feel so stupid. I caught one or two sidelong glances, and was sure they thought I was weird, a voyeur almost, the way I smiled and watched, yet stayed hovering on the outskirts.

I turned back to Jenny, thinking to myself, *Don't ruin your chances. Don't ruin everything.* I took a deep breath, and said, 'I guess I'm getting used to it. Yeah, I guess I could get to like it, maybe.'

She cocked her head. 'You know, I've just figured out why you stand out so much.' I braced myself again. 'It's because you're so tall. It's like you're floating a couple of inches above the floor, kind of ghostly.' She chewed at one side of her bottom lip. 'How come you're on your own so much?'

The words were out before I could think. 'I don't make friends that easily.'

She didn't seem at all perturbed. 'I'm sick of everyone in my classes. They're all backwards. It's a relief to meet someone new.' She gave one of her running laughs—and, as I felt the tangled nerves unloosen all along my body, there was a simultaneous lightening of the room. Jenny had the kind of laugh that would turn heads in public places: the kind of laugh that would have strangers want to join in, despite themselves. It seemed layered with delicious enigma. Back then I felt so privileged to be chosen by her. But now, as I sit here with my hands around a half-filled glass and stare at an empty chair across the room, I wonder whether she had been feeling isolated as well: had found herself adrift, kicking around the edges of those defined clusters of friends, waiting for some-one to notice.

I asked her once, much later, why she had singled me out, at the beginning.

'You were so quiet. I always want to know what quiet people are thinking. I figure they must have deep, dark secrets.'

Incredulous, I crowed, 'But I thought *you* were mysterious!'

'Me? But I talk all the time! I reckon it's more of a challenge to get a quiet person to talk. I figure they must really trust you if they do.'

I have a clear picture of her then, as she leaned forward and moved her face in towards mine until our eyelashes just touched.

'Do you trust me?' she whispered.

I blinked, and we stared at each other for several seconds. I focused on a tiny brown fleck that I'd just discovered floated in the green of one of her irises.

'I can see a little me in your eyes,' she said.

I blinked again.

'Shy girl,' she teased. Then I shot forward, and managed to nip her on the nose with my teeth. She fell backwards on the bed, squealing.

After our first encounter, I half expected not to see her again. I looked for her on the way to school the next day, and at break. All through the classes before lunch I dreaded the prospect of going up to the school library on my own to do homework. All the courage I'd shown in my first three weeks of school was weakened by having had that brief taste of companionship. For a terrible few minutes, walking across the quadrangle, I felt I was collecting girls' stares like hooked burrs: hard-shelled seeds that wanted to germinate, push their stiff little blades under my skin. But as I walked, forcing myself to focus above their heads, I saw Jenny shoulder aside some third formers.

'Hiya,' she said. 'I've figured out which form room you must be in. Are you busy for lunch?'

She slipped an arm through mine, seeming to relish the audience which I'd loathed. My heart skipped and jumped, dancing in the fancy footwork of a girl flying through a game of elastics. The light in Jen's eyes intensified, and we laughed together, both knowing how to make it seem as if we shared a pact. Swinging our hair, we were tossing away all those clinging, schoolyard stares. They flaked from me, shrivelling and desiccated, shaken free like dust. Some small, closed part of me began to expand and open.

I went back to Jenny's house again that afternoon. I wasn't too keen on witnessing another encounter between her and Marion, but Jenny promised me her stepmother would be at work.

When we arrived, Jonathon was just heading out.

'Howdy,' he said.

'Hi.' I looked at my feet, but the little hairs on my bare forearms lifted in the shifting current of air as he passed. I took a furtive look at Jenny, but she didn't seem to notice. I hugged my arms to myself and followed her to her room.

Jen and I went through her record collection—we agreed on Joy Division—and decided to do homework together. She helped me with my maths, and I was impressed by the way she managed to power through everything without really trying. Later, we lazed around, talking, Jenny stretched out on the floor while I curled up on my side on her bed. We talked about which of our teachers we preferred, which subjects were our best, which girls in our form rooms we thought were stuck up, which of the Seniors we most wished we could be like:

'Nancy Martin. She's sooooooo beautiful. She could be a French film star, I swear. And she's so cool: she helps to organise those anti-vivisection marches, you know. I've seen her at pickets.'

'No, I think she's too snooty. You can tell she thinks she's great. Simone Draper's better. She looks like Rickie Lee Jones. Or Carly Simon. I bet she plays guitar.'

Just then we heard keys at the front door, and Marion called out, 'Anyone home?' She was much earlier than expected, and Jenny started up guiltily, slipping out of her room. I heard her greet Marion in a sing-song voice and offer to make her a fresh pot of coffee. Marion's voice deflated, with happy exhaustion this time. 'Oh, Jen, that'd be lovely.' They talked on for a while, chatting about Marion's day helping out at Jen's father Gerald's office. I could hear Marion becoming more and more fractious: ' . . . and the other two secretaries—silly tarts—seem to think your father and I are just idling away our time together, so they both end up taking off for lunch at the same time, and I'm left minding the phones and reception on my own! I didn't get a break all day, because of course when they got back Gerald and I were behind on the checking, and I could hardly let him down.

That's the trouble when you're working for someone you're close to . . . it's much harder, you know . . .'

Jenny was sympathetic at first, but as Marion circled back to the same complaints, she said, 'Well, why don't you just hunt for another job?'

There was a silence.

'What's that supposed to mean?'

'If you don't enjoy it at Dad's, why don't you do something else?'

'I don't think I like your tone, Jennifer.'

I found myself defensively bringing my knees up to my chest as I listened.

Jenny's tone did change then, tightening with anxiety. 'I didn't mean it like that, I just meant . . .'

'Look, Jennifer. I don't really need a fourteen-year-old's advice on how to lead my life.'

'Okay, okay, it's *okay*. I was only trying to help.' There was a pause, then Jenny's disheartened, reluctant, 'Coffee's ready.'

She must have poured out three mugs, because Marion asked, 'Who's that for?'

'Marie.'

'What?'

'She's in my room. We're doing homework.'

I moved to the far end of the bed, pushing myself up against a wall, as if I could pass through it and set it between us like a shield. I didn't actually hear what was said next—they had lowered their voices, I suppose—but Jenny told me that Marion took the full cup she was offered—and launched it into the sink. Hot coffee geysered everywhere, the cup handle broke, and Marion slammed out of the kitchen. Jenny was still red and baffled by her injustice when she elbowed open the bedroom door.

'What got into her?'

Jenny made an acid-drop mouth at me. 'What gets into her

most of the time? She's always going off at me like that. Throwing things, breaking things. She's a total bitch.' She handed me both mugs, then dropped heavily onto the bed. I just managed not to spill anything as the mattress rebounded from the impact. We drank our coffee quietly for a while, and Jenny seemed calmer. I asked her if she was okay. She didn't answer me. The silence began to fill my mouth like sand. Eventually, half thinking she might turn her temper on me, I tried once more, asking how long Marion had lived with them and what she was really like. Jenny stared sullenly at the toes of her shoes for a moment, then sighed noisily.

She said that Marion had married Gerald when she was only twenty, after Jenny and the boys' mother had died. Marion hadn't done the seventh form at school, but had found a job as a receptionist just before she turned seventeen. She'd been a champion squash and tennis player as a teenager—had played in the girls' singles for each sport, and in the tennis doubles and mixed doubles at national level. She'd even been selected to accompany a secondary schools' tour to Australia when she was sixteen. But Marion's mother wouldn't allow her to go. The school and a local club found separate sponsorship money for her, and the trip was only for six weeks, but her mother—elderly, widowed and restrictive—had said she was too young. 'What do you want with going abroad at your age? I need you here.' Marion had moved out as soon as she could. She hadn't played competitive sport since.

I was incredulous. 'But why not?'

Jenny didn't answer, absorbed by her own account or deliberately not answering—I couldn't tell. She did say that Marion hadn't contacted her mother since she had left home. After two or three years, she had ended up working for Jenny's father, and that was how they met. She still did relief days at his accountancy business, or helped him out in the evenings if he had to work late. Mainly, she looked after the house.

'Can you imagine that?' Jenny said. 'I mean, get a life.'

I didn't understand her. My lips and fingers were tingling slightly, as if the blood had to warm back into them. All Marion's ambitions destroyed by her own *mother*? I was horrified. I stared at Jenny. 'What do you mean?'

'All she does is watch TV or help my Dad. Why can't she do something real? All his friends are her friends, too. She's got none of her own.'

'You think she's lonely?'

Jenny shrugged.

'Maybe she's happy doing what she does.' I was groping aimlessly for suggestions. 'I mean, she's chosen it, hasn't she?'

Jenny briefly narrowed her eyes at me, as if she were trying to decipher some tiny detail up close. Then, deciding, she crooked her finger, so I bent my head a little nearer. She lowered her voice, but the tone was stabbing, prodding me into sharing her scandalised reaction. The words said, *There. Now what do you think?* At the same time, she was testing them, testing herself, testing me.

'She can't have children.'

'Oh?'

'She's tried. *Four* miscarriages. All boys.'

Why did Jenny say it like that? The words almost sizzled on her tongue, snipping like hot cooking fat.

'Miscarriages?' I said, stupidly. 'Can you know the sex, if it's a miscarriage?'

'Oh, yes.' Now Jenny sounded plumply satisfied and worldly. 'Didn't you know that? I thought you would, what with your Mum being a nurse and everything.' She began to twist her hair into a thick swathe, draping it forward over one shoulder. 'Marion had real funerals for all of them. The coffins looked like they were made of icing from a wedding cake, and they were as small as shoeboxes. My Dad wouldn't go to the last ceremony. They had a big bust-up about that.'

Miscarriages. Four tiny grey boys, their faces too aged, their eyes closed, hands on their tummies, were carried away, by mistake, in white boxes on wheels. I hardly knew what to say next. But I swallowed, and asked, 'Did she try again after that?'

Jenny shook her head. 'That was part of their row. Dad said enough was enough. "It's cruel on everyone to try," he said.'

The four little grey babies lined up over and over in my mind. 'Oh my God. Poor *Marion*,' I said.

Jenny blinked. It seemed I hadn't given the expected reaction. I had momentarily taken Marion's side. And Jenny had begun to move past trying to understand her. All she wanted was an ally.

I asked Jenny that afternoon what it was like when Marion first moved in. I tried to think of how I would have reacted if my father had brought home a new wife, much younger than him. And even in imagining, I felt a six- or seven-year-old's hot, sickening jealousy—as if it would have meant another older sister to compete with: for turns on his knee, for the short supply of attention he could spare from his work. As if it would have meant not just the loss of my mother but the loss of part of my father as well. I tried to magnify and multiply that feeling, struggling to understand why Jenny harboured so little sympathy for her stepmother.

'Marion was okay at first, I guess,' Jenny said slowly, as if she were reconsidering. 'She'd buy us little presents, take us to the movies. I remember that.' She frowned, concentrating. 'First of all, when she arrived, she'd want to play with my hair all the time, have me sit in her lap before I went to bed, which I'd accept if Dad was around, because I knew he wanted so badly for me to like her. But I didn't want her hands on me.' Jenny looked embarrassed. 'She hardly ever did that to Gareth and Jonathon, which made me feel guilty. Like I was hurting them. I wanted her to leave me alone, stop all her fussing and touching.' Jenny glanced at me. 'But then, I remember, she stopped trying to hug and kiss me when she first got pregnant—and I had a *weird* kind of feeling. Wondering why she'd stopped, even though I'd always tried to move away from her. Really weird.' Jenny shook her head, the way she would have if she'd been talking about someone she used to know who'd always worried her: say a funny kid who'd lived down the road, whom she would never have chosen to play with if circumstances hadn't made her do so—not her sort of person at all.

I was afraid of giving the wrong reaction again, so tried to echo what she had said. 'It must have been awful when she kept on at you like that.'

She rolled her eyes at me, agreeing. 'Yeah. And now it seems like she just hates me most of the time.' She pushed a hand through her hair. Blushing slightly, she thought for a while. 'But you know, there are times when, completely randomly, she'll go and act as if we've got this special "womanly" closeness.' Jenny squinted a little as she said this, and her shoulders hunched forwards. 'She even tried to talk to me about *periods* the other day.'

I butted in, enormously relieved: this was something I could relate to. 'Oh, my Mum does that all the time! I mean, all the time!'

Jenny hardly paused to listen.

'Yeah, but I mean, Marion is like, "Jenny, I want to make sure you know about your *monthly*." And I'm, like, "My monthly what? Bus pass? And she goes all pleased-looking, as if we're sharing this really special moment, and she says, "Every month, a girl's body gets ready to . . .", and so then I interrupt her, I'm *so* embarrassed. Does she think I'm a moron, or what? I mean, doesn't she remember the letter she signed when I was in form two? When there was a talk, girls only, and we had to get permission to go along? So I say, "Oh, I know all about that. You don't have to tell me." And she looks down at her hands, going pick, pick, pick, at her fingernails, it's a habit she has, it drives me nuts, this really annoying little clicking sound all the time, and she says, "It's just that I've noticed that you still haven't started." Oh, I was so grossed out. What is she doing? Inspecting all my laundry or something? And she goes, "When you do, you must understand that you just have to ask me to get you anything you need with the weekly groceries." That really grossed me out, too.'

I didn't quite understand this point, but I wrinkled up my nose as if I did.

'And she also said that if I was worried about being late, she could take me to Dr Clements. And I'm like, *no way*, Dr Clements is a total lech, and I don't want Marion sitting round listening in to all my business. And you want to know the most bizarre thing of all?' She stopped for a proper breath at last, and to check whether I did really want to hear.

'What?'

'I just started yesterday!' She seemed to find that a great coup, and in a complete change of mood now, leaned back her head and gave an enormous stage laugh. Then we were both giggling —Jenny told me I'd turned purple, and soon she had as well— each new fit of giggles triggered by the last. It was an enormous release.

Yet her earlier intensity had finalised something. From then on we could talk about anything, especially the things Jenny wouldn't discuss with Marion. We became bonded: tied together by confidences, admissions, secrets and promises. The telling, and the knowledge that we wouldn't retell such things to anyone, was like a private ritual of communion and absolution.

That day I walked home so exhilarated I found myself experiencing sensations I hadn't felt since I was a little kid, when, deliriously happy, I could project myself into imaginary backflips all along the pavement, or I'd feel that I was hanging upside down from my toes, suspended in the sky, swinging in great arcs backwards and forwards. At last I had found someone of my own.

As I ran over everything we'd talked about, knowing my family would ask me where I'd been, one or two moments of Jen's unhappiness touched at the edges of my mood, slowing me down to a dawdle. There was a lot I'd have to leave out if I told anyone else about what we'd discussed. The way Jen's eyes had changed . . . I'd never seen that before . . . I shook myself briefly, telling myself to cut it out, quit filling myself with the spooks.

But as Jenny's confessions should have foreshadowed, our friendship was to grow more and more embroiled in complexities that my initial euphoria had in fact overlooked. As I grew to know Jenny and Marion better, I learned to fear Marion's unpredictable temper. And it certainly was Jenny who received the worst of it. Maybe her manner made Marion less tolerant of her, but to me the contrast with Marion's treatment of the boys was excruciating.

'Oh, sweetie,' she'd say to them, looking at them guiltily, hungrily, after she'd snapped, sometimes even reaching out for a hug. 'You big men can take a bit of criticism, eh?' But after an argument with Jen, Marion would carry on giving her monosyllabic ice-queenly commands for hours afterwards: 'Get that for me.' 'Oh, don't start.'

Gareth took this all in silence, but Jonathon obviously loathed it. His eyes would appear to fill with clear heat, his neck moving as if his grey school collar pinched, and he'd look over to his father, pleading for rescue. Sometimes he even voiced it with a questioning 'Dad?'

It's odd the way details like these have stayed with me. I wonder if I remember them only because I'm so influenced by what happened to Jen later—because now it's easier to join up certain distinct patches of memory to make a believable whole. In themselves, particular incidents might seem insignificant, but I'm compelled to re-enter even the most uneventful of days we spent together, in an effort to understand how everything ended:

to see if anything was foretold in the daily circumstances of our friendship. Were they really so ordinary?

Like the day Jen rushed to the front door as her father came home, and called out that she'd come top in French, with 93 percent. I stood there, goofy and grinning, expecting Gerald to hug her; instead, Marion came up and stepped carefully between them. With an imploring look she reached up and slowly, lingering, she kissed Gerald on the mouth. Jenny dropped back, jostled aside by Marion's crowding body and hands.

On another occasion, I was asked to stay for an evening meal to celebrate Jen's glowing mid-term report. As Gerald made a toast, the little patches of red that showed just above his trim, greying beard seemed flagged there on his cheekbones in specific celebration.

'You're going to be my high-flying career girl, aren't you, Jen?' he said. 'Marks like that, you'll be able to do anything you want. Better than any of us, I'll bet.'

He raised his glass to me, then to Jen, took a deep pull on his wine, and held the mouthful for a few seconds, to savour its mild smoke. He leaned back in his chair as if he were holding Jen at arm's length so that he could appraise her more fully. 'New generation of women, eh?' he said. He smiled, and for a single, suspended instant, I could see there was a cocoon of mutual feeling that held just Jenny and her father. Then Marion shoved back her chair from the table and, with a clash of plates, began loading a tray.

'Leave that, Marion, love,' Gerald waved a hand. 'Someone else can do it later.' He moved to refill her wine glass. Marion stopped, her back to him. Then, with a heavy push of one shoulder at the dining room door, she left the room.

I saw a series of glances scatter around the table, quick and helpless as collapsing dominoes. There was a splintering crash from the kitchen. Gareth and Jonathon, who had been good-naturedly hassling Jenny during the meal ('So, Brown-nose, did you cheat?' 'What's A stand for? Airhead?'), instantly took the cue to leave the table, both skulking off to the hallway and the opposite end of the house. Gerald dropped a crumpled serviette and swung his way to the kitchen. After a few seconds of listening for what would eventuate, Jenny whispered to me.

'Let's go.'

We lifted our chairs quietly, and stole out into the hallway. The kitchen door was just a little ajar as we came past. I looked in, despite myself. With shards of crockery still littered on the floor, Gerald was behind Marion, massaging her shoulders as she stood stiffly, head lowered, at the kitchen sink. I saw him take a step closer, but she jerked from him, aggressively. Insistent, he pressed his lips to her ear. Then, too readily, in one movement, Marion's body seemed to pour into the mould of his as her head tilted back. Her hand, nails digging, went to the soft creaminess of his throat, while his mouth sealed over hers, which had parted for him. Together they seemed to struggle for air—or was it to hold the other one down, under the surface of whatever bound them together? I hurried past, away, away from it. Away from the viciousness of its quick succession upon Gerald's celebration toast to Jenny. It had made me feel the sense of alarm and self-questioning guilt that I've felt since at other scenes—chanced upon around a street corner, outside a pub, on the platform of a tube station. Fists, throats, lips, something dark running a face, something dark running the pavement, someone stopped, or someone pursued, running in the dark . . . the flashlit, fragmented scene that breaks loose and falling from the full story. It's as if, in witnessing something, I've been made complicit to it. Yet I did try to help Jenny. I did.

My understanding of her home would finally grow from such scenes which disturbed or leaked into my view. At first, I tried to cajole Jen into seeing Marion differently. With little phrases, suggestions, cautions, questions—like my mother, I suppose— I tried to nudge her towards making peace. But as I saw Marion's dissatisfaction deflected more and more on to Jen, and as I saw Gerald floundering between a passive disagreement with Marion and siding grimly with her, I learned that peace could never be effected through Jenny's diplomacy alone.

It was always Marion who meted out the discipline and punishments—curfews, chores, dos and don'ts. (A plate thrown against a wall when Jonathon came home late. A door nearly slammed on Gareth's hand, for nothing worse than his introversion, his refusal to be goaded. A glass of wine tossed into Jenny's face . . .) If Gerald disagreed with her, all he did was fade into his clothes, erasing himself from the scene. His face—like Jenny's and Jonathon's the first time I saw Marion—simply stilled. Then he'd withdraw to his workshop, his garden, or to his office, to 'sort out paperwork'. And when he did side with Marion the disturbing energy of that scene in the kitchen would inhabit him again, as if he were desperate to clutch onto her, stop himself from missing his foothold. Sometimes he'd baby Marion, nurse her with one arm around her shoulders, saying, 'My girl okay now?'

He didn't seem to realise that the way he gave in to Marion pitched her against Jenny. Who was really his little girl? It still sickens me, the way Gerald's relationship with Marion blinded him to the point where he couldn't see how he conceded to her at the expense of his children. Maybe dread of losing someone a second time, after Jenny's mother died so young, shadowed all his other love.

Often, after their fights, Jenny was the one who made the first attempt to patch things up. She would bake, clean the bathroom or the oven, even buy Marion a magazine, and Marion appeared to accept the overtures. To start with, I believed in these truces. I even thought that Marion and Jenny's guilt about the clashes might mean that there was a small but broadening appreciation between them. But soon I saw that these reconciliations were only ever carried out in front of Gerald, engineered so that he was there as a witness. They made their gestures for him, not for one another.

I remember the last time I saw Jenny make a genuine effort to deny that she and Marion weren't in a constant, simmering state of antagonism. It was also in our first year of knowing each other. We'd gone Christmas shopping together, and Jen had saved up pocket money to buy an expensive perfume for Marion. She pointed out the frosted glass bottle, its top flared out slightly to suggest wings, and she said to the shop assistant, 'It's for my Mum.' I felt my curiosity prickle.

'That's really nice, Jen,' I said—with an emphasis that she knew was a question.

'It's Christmas, isn't it?' she replied, pushing away my curiosity like a cat from her lap. But she bit her lip as the assistant crisply tucked the bottle into thin, holly-printed paper.

Jen insisted on stopping to check all her purchases twice on the way home, as if they might somehow have vanished. I don't know what made her try so hard that year—though I do remember her asking me several times what I usually did for Christmas. Hope stoked by all the seasonal convictions, the cards and icons, mother and child, lined up in shop windows, display cases, even on our separate family mantelpieces. Maybe she just wanted to believe that her family could act out the myth for once: that she could achieve some final sense of appeasement.

I didn't contact Jenny on Christmas Day, but was first to the phone when it rang early on Boxing Day.

'Hello?'

'Hello?' From those two syllables alone I could hear that Jenny was dammed up with tears.

'Hey, Jen. Is everything all right?'

'Everything sucks.'

'Jenny? What's happened?'

'Marion. That's what.'

I leaned against the wall. 'What's she done?'

I could hear Jen's struggle to swallow back her distress, but it came out in a bitter volley. 'She's only had a totally flipped-out screaming fit at me, hasn't she? You'd think I'd be used to it by now.'

'Used to it? God, no. Why should you be?' I flexed my fingers on the handset, trying to think of what I could say without setting her off in floods of tears. 'Look, why don't you come round here? Get away from things for a couple of hours?'

'Can I? You sure?'

'Sure I'm sure. It'd be great to see you.'

Of course it wasn't all great. That day I saw a side of Jen that I suppose I was half consciously trying to ward off. Not from myself, but from her.

When Jen arrived on our doorstep, Dad was a little surprised. To him, Christmas and Boxing Day meant relatives (all of us walled in together like stiff little figures in a diorama), and he assumed that Jenny would be ensconced with hers. Public holidays were one of the few escapes he allowed himself from work, especially since his promotion, but I didn't share the relief. After only a couple of enforced hours with my sisters I had cabin fever.

When the doorbell rang, I leapt, but Dad got there before me.

'Jennifer!' he was a little taken aback. 'Ah, Jennifer—you must have come to rescue us from Marie.'

'I've come at a bad time.'

'Of course not. Hi there, Jen!' Mum was hurrying through to the living room, her tea tray laden. 'Just in time for tea and mince pies. We'll need help eating all this food.'

'Welcome to the house of Christmas spirit,' I said, relieved to have got in a word at last. I reached past Dad to rescue them both from awkwardness, and pulled Jen inside for a hug.

'More Christmassy than my place,' she muttered.

Then Dad clicked. He stepped back, booming, redundantly,

'Yes, yes, join us, Jennifer. Come in.'

I gave him an angelic little smile, and he raised an eyebrow, fractionally, at me.

As Jenny hovered in the corridor, hedging around Lucy's 'Oh, how has *your* Christmas been, Jenny? What did you *get?*' my aunts and uncles began to arrive, the men, as their contribution to the labours of the day, carrying the women's baking: a serious suburban ceremony.

Seeing them through the living room window, Dad announced, 'Here they are, here they are!' as if we'd been waiting for hours, and had even begun asking, 'What if there's been an accident? What if something's happened? What if they can't get to a phone?' I knew they'd probably been parked around the corner for quarter of an hour, waiting patiently, precisely and politely for it to be 'quite the right time yet'. We'd done it ourselves as a family; it drove me mad.

Under the pretence of showing Jenny my presents, she and I managed to slide away.

I was bursting with indignation at the predictability of the day but I realised I'd have to wait to talk to Jenny about it. Close up, her eyelids still looked red and puffy from crying.

I sat down opposite her. 'Things got pretty bad, did they?'

Jen tilted her chin at the ceiling, as if tipping back tears. 'Bloody bitch. I *hate* her.'

She avoided my eyes for several seconds, but then, through quavering stops and starts, I learned that Marion, already well past tipsy by noon, had shouted at Jenny for something trivial— not washing the Christmas roasting pan, when it had been soaking for a whole day. Then she sprayed herself with Jenny's perfume, 'like she was a blowfly trying to commit aerosol suicide', and Jenny, already riled, told Marion it was too strong. Soon, they'd started a slanging match, in the middle of which Marion deliberately swept the scent bottle off the kitchen bench where she'd stacked all her presents. It splintered on their fashionable slate floor. Immediately, Gerald went to comfort Marion—'She didn't like the jewellery he gave her, either, and he was trying to make up'—and he told Jen she was provoking, pushing people to their limits: 'You were goading her, you know you were. You know what upsets her.' On top of all that, one of Jen's usually loyal brothers clumsily tried to make light of it. Gareth said, 'It was probably cheap stuff anyway, Dad. We can get her some more.' But of course I knew Jen had saved for it especially.

'Everyone was against me in some way,' she said. Her expression fought against tears again, a tiny muscle in one cheek trembling with the effort. 'I can never do anything right. I tried—I really did try to make it okay. Oh, God . . .'

I felt pain swell inside me as I watched her face, the feeling growing worse as I felt less and less capable of saying anything to comfort her. I cupped one of her knees briefly in my hand, and we sat there, silent. She picked at her cuticles nervously, pushed up her shirt sleeves, then shifted in her sitting position. I leaned in, listening, thinking she was settling herself so that she could really explain. Which she was, in a way. She wanted me to see. On her left forearm, three thin fish gills. Parallel stripes, red and open. Not deep enough to . . . no, not deliberate in that way—I'm reassuring myself even now, all these years later—but still ugly, fresh, raw.

'*Shit*, Jenny,' I said, misunderstanding. 'Did Marion do that?'

She shook her head.

The strangest feeling came upon me then. A narrowing of the room, a sudden jab in my temples, cold pressure in the veins on the upper insides of my arms. I stared at her.

'Don't look at me like I'm a freak.'

'Jenny, I'm not. I'm not.' And then, more quietly, 'Why did you do it?'

She shook her head again, as if what she was about to say wasn't quite what she meant. As if she still didn't know what she meant.

'Cuts give you something else to think about.'

I couldn't look away from them. 'That doesn't make any sense. You can't hurt yourself just because everyone else is hurting you. You know them hurting you is wrong.' I could hear my voice turning on edge, like metal twisted to deflect harsh light into her eyes, but I couldn't stop it. 'Why would you want to make yourself feel more pain?'

'It's not that I *want* to . . .'

'So how could you do that?'

'I hated myself.'

I slid from where I was sitting beside her on the bed, and knelt down on the floor, my hands on her knees, eyes searching her face. 'Jenny, you can't, you can't. You're so much better than them. You're so much better than anyone I've ever met. You're different, you're brave, you're amazing—' I rambled, pleading with her.

She tipped her head, looked at the cuts, and touched their red lips lightly with her fingers.

'Once I'd done it, I kind of stopped feeling that way. It kind of—woke me up. And so I called you.'

She swept me a brief look of supplication, but then quickly withdrew it.

I dropped my hands from her knees, and sat there on my haunches, knuckles up to my mouth, trying to figure out what to do. I reached up again, and slowly rolled down her shirt sleeve to cover the damage. 'Let's get you past everyone,' I said, 'And into the bathroom.'

Once there, I made her wash the cuts with warm water and a little Dettol. It stung; she leaned back, involuntarily pulling away her arm. Then I dressed the wounds with Savlon cream and gauze. I didn't know if that was the right thing to do, for incisions like that. They scarred later. A mild, candyfloss pink, incongruously innocent.

With a determination I almost didn't recognise in myself,

and that I'm proud of even now, I made Jenny promise: 'Next time you feel like that, call me first. Not afterwards. You have to call me, okay?' Squeezing her other arm, hard. 'Okay?'

She twisted in my grip. 'Okay.'

I searched her face again, and tried to coax her into smiling. 'We'll do some voodoo. We'll make a picture of Marion and cut that up instead.' For a moment I thought she was angry that I'd made such a pathetic suggestion. Instead she gave a quiet, wry huff.

A few times after that, when she came over for shelter after an argument, she did sketch a woman's face. Then, as she talked, she'd puncture it again and again with the nib of her pen, so the paper looked as if it had met a hail of bullets. My cream bedspread had inky stab marks all over it. I kept asking her to let me see her arm, until it had healed over cleanly. Then we didn't mention it again, and I began to think that our talks could always mend things, and that this was part of my meaning for her, of her need for me. And I still believe that. I have to.

That particular Christmas did it for Jenny's efforts
with Marion. She wasn't going to let herself be reduced by her again; she wasn't going to let Marion win. If she ever met Marion's jibes with silence, the retreats were tactical—designed to get what she wanted, but to get it behind Marion's back.

The underlying causes of each separate argument at Jenny's were something I could never quite isolate as a teenager, though early on I always tried to get her to tell me what had happened: what had triggered each one of the rows. I don't think even Jenny knew Marion's reasons for exploding half the time. She would grow vague, but as she grew more vague, more injured, it became clear that my probing was unwelcome, and I soon worked out that I was more sorely needed for the casualties than for analysis. I learned to hold Jenny when she cried, tucking her hair behind her ears, letting her tears run over my index finger, as I held it like a sill under her eyes, until she could laugh at how wet she'd made my hands. When she laughed, my anxiety always dissolved. She'd come to me, needed me, just me, and I'd helped her. I hadn't let her down.

'Fucken bitch,' we'd say, each trying to sound more sinister than the other, drawing it out, sneering, putting all the broken bottles we could muster into just those two words. 'Fahhh- ken bitch.' 'Fahhhhhkin bi-i-i-tch.' Sometimes, when the fights had become really bad, Jenny would push it. She'd ram into walls, crash out of the house, yell in the yard. *'UP YOURS!'* But always as the door slammed shut. Then she'd run around to my place, afraid to go back.

'Can Jenny stay the night? Her parents say it's okay if it's okay by you,' I'd gabble to Mum. 'Of course,' she'd answer. My father had started to greet Jen with pseudo-surprise by then: 'Ah, Jennifer!' he'd say, when she appeared at the dinner table. 'And where have you been over the last forty-eight hours? Can't keep you away from good home cooking, eh?'

By the time she did return home, Gerald would know about the row, and would do all the 'dealing'. Usually he'd give Jenny the wounded look that meant things would be quiet for a while. He'd made some concession to Marion: offered her a shopping trip or a restaurant dinner. Once, though, he grounded Jenny for two weeks. The worst punishment, she said: having to stay in every night. She wasn't even supposed to use the phone, and had to be home by four every afternoon. Each evening, just before dinner, I would cycle to her and post letters to her through the round hole in the birdhouse-shaped letter box that perched on a stake near their front gate. The letters, headed with however many days there were to go until her curfew was over, were written in a series of different colours, decorated with cartoons of Jenny behind black jail bars, her hair drawn in orange felt pen. I signed off, 'I miss you!!!! I wish we could talk!!!!'

She had been grounded after Marion saw her walking home with one of Jonathon's friends. Apparently they'd stayed outside the house for ages, talking.

'Then I said we could pash,' Jenny told me.

'You what?'

'Pash, you know. God, Marie. Like French kiss. Like passionate.'

54

'Oh. Did you like him, then?'

'Not much. But I just *knew* Marion was twitching the net curtains. Still watching me like I'm a little kid. So we snogged. And then when I went inside to help cook dinner Marion just turned on me. Practically spat at me, called me a little slut.' She imitated Marion: 'Right out there in the street! You're out to give this family a filthy name. You looked so *cheap*."'

On and on Marion went, until Jenny, moving a pot of cooked peas to the sink to drain them, just snapped. Dropped the pot. Boiling water leapt from the saucepan, riding up Marion's leg, badly scalding the calf through her trousers. The skin blistered, and peeled off later in a wet, brown film, 'like the top layer off hot milk', Jen said. 'But I still couldn't say sorry.'

That frightened her the most.

'You didn't mean to do it,' I said. 'It was an accident.'

Her expression modulated into self-loathing. 'I'd hoped it would get her. I wanted to hurt her.' A small, curling wisp of horror smoked up from her words. 'I'm just like her.'

'No,' I said, 'No. No, you're not.'

Jenny did all she could to avoid another grounding, and so our rooms became our sanctuaries, the secrets in them a subtler rebellion against Marion. As Jenny and I withdrew together, I began to separate myself even more from my own family, treasuring the idea that Jenny understood me far better than they did.

We began to keep secrets simply for the sake of nobody else knowing about them. Initially, it was completely innocent. It just started off with things like the books we checked out from the library—like *Lady Chatterley's Lover*, as soon as we heard in English that it had been banned. Although that was the only real interest we had in it, we took a conceited pride in believing that Marion, and my sisters, were a bit thick. 'It's literature,' said Jenny. 'They'd want to know where the recipes were.' And then there were the magazines we'd buy, with articles about men and menstruation, their slick covers in neon contrast to Marion's *Better Homes* fare.

In the park on Friday and Saturday nights we came to try cigarettes (I hated the fiery grit in my lungs, and gave up after a few attempts), then mixing together non-prescription cough syrups, eating nutmeg, dissolving Disprin in coke, and taking No-Doze caffeine tablets because they were rumoured to make you speed. Eventually, we convinced Jenny's brothers to smuggle us alcohol, as the four of us gathered on the kids' swings or the park benches.

On these occasions, Gareth was friendly enough, but distracted; Jenny and I were still little kids to him, and he always had somewhere else to be. I got the feeling that he thought us a liability and had to be watched, or have our hands held. Still, we felt honoured when he came to the park with us, as if he were a kind of elusive local celebrity.

Jonathon was different. I remember one night—Jenny's birthday, it was—when we sat in the park, our backs propped up against the rough bark of the pines around its far perimeter, and passed around a bottle of sweet ginger wine. Jonathon struck up a series of questions, as if he and I were involved in a slow, summer volley. What's your Dad's name, what does your Mum do, do you have any brothers or sisters? I began to sense, as I watched his relaxed silhouette, that if he'd had more time to slow down, to hang back from his motocross friends, he might have become interested . . . It scared me a little, even this mild undercurrent; yet after that night, I discovered a curiosity that both did—and didn't —want to unfurl each time I saw him.

Encounters like these were always brief and clandestine, but through them Gareth's and Jonathon's company became less nerve-wracking. In fact, their very 'ordinariness' was intriguing. I was fascinated to find they worried about the same things we did: grades, friends, teachers, home. At Jenny's place, I'd find an excuse to leave by the back door when I knew Jonathon was busy in the yard—but then I'd rush through the gate without looking at him. And when we weren't all washed in the same vague haze as the full moon, he went back to his comings and goings, his motocross and his sullenness with Marion, busy being sixteen.

When Jenny and I weren't hanging around at the park or the beach, I naturally tended to encourage her back to my place, where at least there was little overt friction. That said, if Mum had found out we'd been drinking, she'd have had a 'spack attack', as Heather and Lucy called it. She was open and accepting about many things, but whenever there was something that frightened her—like when Heather's first boyfriend drove her home after drinking four cans of beer, or when Jenny came over in a green 'Adi-hash' t-shirt she'd borrowed from Gareth—Mum would start. With how she knew she could *trust* her children, that we'd always *talked*—and then there would be her lectures. Real ones, I mean. When we all had to gather in the living room, and Mum would bring out her illustrations: pamphlets and horrible pictures from her nursing textbooks. Somehow, Dad always managed to absent himself from these sessions—a fact which added to their seriousness, as if it were a strategy that my parents had agreed upon in private consultation. I'd send him pleading looks as he left the room, but he'd set his expression in a way that said, 'It's best you girls hear this sort of thing from your mother.' Later, at the appropriate moment, he'd come back in, rubbing his hands, and ask anyone if they wanted cocoa before bed. Much as I dreaded those sessions, I suppose I paid them a kind of grudging respect. They made me see that Mum was genuinely hurt: it was as if she felt abandoned by us. She really did care. At the time, I felt a secret, sulky satisfaction that—if I was the one in trouble— I'd proven myself independent, *different*. But this was always undermined by the strangely protective tenderness her anxiety could surprise in me, and by the guilt I felt when I realised I'd worried her. 'I should have known how she'd react . . .' I'd resolve to try not to sadden her that way again. And now I'm convinced that these motherly conferences helped to make me that little bit more wary than Jen.

Jen of course had much more to fight against. Marion was becoming more and more prone to drinking. I was used to their Friday nights, when Gerald was usually home early, and their shared bottle of wine seemed to dull the acuity of Marion's temper. She could even be funny: mimic TV presenters like a parrot, and sometimes she'd smile at me as we shot past the living room, catching me off guard by saying a full sentence: 'Oh, Marie, you again—it's nice for Jen to have a friend over— not much company for her in a house of boys!' For a brief moment she'd behave as if she, Jenny and I had something in common. Perhaps she made other attempts to forge some connection with us. I failed or did not care to notice.

When I told Joss about all this, he asked me if I'd ever sat down with Marion on her own. 'Not really,' I'd said, surprised that he'd focused on her, and a little annoyed that he'd missed my point. 'I mean I was a teenager. I wouldn't have known what to say to her.'

I was there only for Jenny. In fact, I think I disliked Marion more for the way she still sought these moments of connection and tried to work under my skin, when I'd seen her belittle Jenny so often. Because there were other occasions when, even at four o'clock in the afternoon, she would be sitting in the lounge in front of TV, cushions packed around her for comfort, a cask of wine within arm's reach. When she drank this early she could grow irritable—there seemed to be a certain degree of red wine that made her relaxed and happy, a degree that made her crabby and a degree that made her doze off. I learned to anticipate the various levels, and to hope to see her dozing, curled up inside a nest of cushions as the TV chattered on. Then, Jenny's shoulders would visibly lose their tension, unlocking again from where they'd tried to close in, like a bird's wings huddled up for warmth. I'd be grateful, as well, that we had escaped a grilling—although as the sight of Marion slumbering on the couch became more regular, I also experienced a hurried, half-conscious scrawling of some other emotion. At the time, I just attributed it to my nervousness that she might wake up, tired and crotchety; my confusion and concern concealed themselves again as soon as we'd left the room and had immersed ourselves in homework and gossip. I was still too self-preoccupied to ask any whys and hows: probably the nearest I came was to think: *'Look at Marion. There she goes again.'*

Such complacency about Marion's drinking came to an end one night when she came into Jenny's room, looking for someone to go out to the corner store for her. Marion heaved open the door, leaning against it as if it had swung too quickly. Jen and I both jumped, our conversation cut off as abruptly as if a plug had been kicked out of the wall. Marion took a few moments to focus, then she went out again, into the hallway, calling for Gerald. When she came back, she was holding the dog's leash which usually hung from a hook near the oilskins.

Then everything happened as if we were under water—slow and clogged. I didn't even realise that what Marion had focused on was a packet of cigarettes on Jen's desk. Marion smoked: that was no big deal; and I assumed Jenny's pack would go unnoticed. But then, I still expected Marion to make some kind of sense.

Marion advanced, lifted her arm, then struck Jenny across the shins with the metal catch. Then she pulled the leash back again. I scrambled to my feet. Jenny doubled over, crying out, and as Marion wrapped the leather strap around her hand for a better grip, I moved between them.

'Don't!' My voice cramped in my throat.

Gerald appeared in the doorway. At his appalled *'What's going on?'* Marion wound up the leather strap, trembling. She picked up the cigarettes from Jenny's desk, and tossed them at him. Gerald caught them with one hand, and looked at them... double checking. As he crumpled the packet in his fist, all he said was, *'Jenny.'* She tucked up her legs, cradling her shins with her hands, shielding them from his sight, and watched him, her face washed of colour. He came over—I sucked in a short breath—but his hand rested briefly on her head.

'You're cleverer than that, my girl.'

'Than what? Marion smokes,' Jenny said.

Gerald avoided Jenny's eyes then; he gripped Marion's shoulder, turned her, and led her from the room. I could tell that he thought I was the equivalent of a public audience, and didn't want the scene to continue in front of me. I went over to Jenny, and unpeeled her hands from her shins. As I bent over her, my own sweat swept up to me from my clothes. It was strong, like burnt hazelnuts, mixed with roast coffee powder. The weals on Jenny's shins were still white, but flecks of red appeared as I inspected them.

'They're okay,' Jenny said, but she drew her legs away from me.

When I brought up the incident again, a few days later, Jenny was dismissive.

'Marion flipped out. She really thought for a minute that I was the dog—she used exactly the same voice.'

I stared at her. It took me a while to interpret Jenny's sass. Her humour was a defence: one that was being eroded even as it was built, like the moat dug around a child's sand castle that fills with the tide, floods and eventually gives way, allowing the whole castle to succumb.

'It's okay, Marie. I told Dad that if she does it again, I'm going to the school counsellor.' Her eyes glittered with laughter. 'Got given extra pocket money after that.'

Mum always beamed at the sight of Jen. She was thrilled that she had 'relaxed' me, that I wasn't always scribbling behind a closed door, as I had been in my first year of high school, marinating in the stuffy air of my bedroom, healthy colour leaching from my skin as I filled exercise book after exercise book with facts and solutions. Mum told me quite openly that she thought Jen had become a 'delightful influence' on me.

Hearing Mum's voice again, in my mind's ear, triggers affection for her which I didn't often show as a teenager. And it makes me ask, how could I hope to understand what happened to Jenny and me without tracking my mother's—and my father's—voices as well? From this distance, everyone seems far more intimately bound together than I would have accepted then. Voices lead into voices: it's like the picture puzzles I had as a child, where my crayon had to follow one winding route from among a tangle of intersecting paths: 'Try to get Jack Horner back to his delicious plum pie: which corners should he turn?'

One thing my mother wasn't so pleased about was Jenny's sway on my wardrobe. She thought Jenny's short skirts would be a red rag to all the 'bad men' in town. Once, she called out to my father to 'Come here and take a look at your daughter.' He came out of the living room, glanced at me, then sauntered over to the hallway mirror, where he smoothed down his hair like the Fonz on TV. Eyeballing her in the reflection, he drawled, 'Heyyy, coool.' She looked furious, as if he'd muffed some plan of action that she'd gone over with him countless times. He came across and patted her on the behind, saying, 'Healthy rebellion, sweetheart, healthy.' That drove her mad, his way of caressing her during a disagreement. I slipped away, secretly pleased that Dad seemed able to have the final word.

There was often this undercurrent of humour between me and my father. Mum was the one I could confide in, the one who patiently explained things; Dad was the one who turned them into a joke, who'd kid with me or share a quick, private smile over some issue to do with my sisters—though I always harboured the thought that he loved them best. Dad was also the one who delivered real punishment. Smacking us for thieving the change from his pockets, sending us to our rooms for fighting, setting us chores for swearing, grounding Heather and Lucy once for coming home an hour late from a double date, and banning me from watching TV for two weeks when I pierced my ears without asking permission. For a while, he took to torturing my sisters' boyfriends whenever they phoned, answering their 'Is Heather there?' 'Is Lucy home?' with, 'Yes, she is. Thank you for asking'—and then hanging up. My sisters cried out at him, 'Dad, you're so *embarrassing!* He'll *never* phone again!' To which the response was, 'If he's really keen, and worth your time, he'll call back. If he doesn't call back, he's a spineless wimp, and I've saved you the pain of getting rid of him later.' When Mum challenged him on Heather's and Lucy's behalf, he said, 'I just know how an adolescent boy's mind works, Claire, and I can tell you, it's not pleasant.'

'You! You told me you didn't have a *single* girlfriend until you were twenty!'

'I didn't say it wasn't for want of thinking about it.' Then Dad batted his eyelids, and nuzzled his weekend-stubbly chin into her bobbed brown hair. Which made me embarrassed, curious about their history, yet finally unable to cope with both emotions at once: 'Oh *gross*, you guys! Just go to your room!'

Often, after Jenny had gone home, and if my mother found me leafing through a magazine in my room, she'd bring me tea or coffee on our battered tin tray. Then she'd perch on the edge of my bed, staying for half an hour or more. I wanted to resist her visits, thinking she might be prying into the things Jenny and I talked about together. Yet I also knew that Mum loved to unwind over tea and gossip after a hospital shift. Besides, sometimes she did offer confidences that I'd want to store up and report to Jenny later: Mum had always sworn to tell me and my sisters *anything you might ever want to know about anything. You only have to ask.*

Mum had been the youngest child in a family of four—three boys and her, the only girl—and she had always felt out of place. As if to make up for those years of lost warmth, she clutched us tightly to her, not wanting us to feel islanded, or even frightened, as she said she sometimes had as a girl.

'I knew almost nothing,' she confessed. 'All I was told was that boys outside the family could get you into trouble, and they mustn't reach past your knee. I thought I might have a baby when my first boyfriend touched my breasts, and I cried right then and there.'

'Oh, Mum!' I was half horrified, half intrigued.

'He got a terrible fright. Wouldn't touch me again—was sure he'd get beaten up by my brothers if they found out I'd been upset. My best friend, Kerrie, told me not to be such a little fool, and explained a bit. I was so *angry* with my mother for not educating me that I just about resolved then and there that I'd be a nurse, so I could find out everything else she hadn't told me.' She would always laugh when she told me that. 'Of course, it wasn't for many more years that I met your father, and I'd been hurt before then, so I'd almost begun to believe my parents were right about the dangers of men.'

'You'd been hurt?' I'd prompt—but to my exasperation, she would deliberately gloss over that story.

'I'll tell you another time. I met your father, and —well! Put him next to my brothers, you couldn't find more of a contrast. They were always fighting each other, drinking, smashing cars, in trouble with the police. Dad used to say, "Just let them be boys, they'll knock the edges off each other . . .."' She would trail off then, thinking.

I'd never met my uncles—two were overseas, and one had died in a farming accident before I was born—but since moving, I'd managed to fuse my mental images of them with two sons of a car mechanic—acquaintances of Jenny's brothers—who worked at one end of their road. The Barry Boys. They were known by most of the kids our age. Like my uncles in their day, they had a kind of small-scale fame as the local louts or hoons: what my father would call 'nasty pieces of work'. They were both tall, lean, wore cracked leather, and it seemed that their faces, hands and hair were always filmed with a thin layer of motor oil. Jenny had announced once that she thought the taller brother, Bruce, was good-looking. She'd return their greetings if we had to walk past their end of her road, and she took a kind of pride in their slow, questioning 'Giddays'. I'd tense as Jenny lingered to talk to them, and avoided them at all costs if I was on my own. Whenever my mother described my uncles, I'd see the Barrys, and didn't feel like asking her much more about her brothers. I wanted to keep away from them, even in imagination.

'But *Don*,' my mother would carry on, when her thoughts led back to my father. 'He was quiet, never argued. And he and I used to talk—real talks, you know, about people—my patients and our families—a way I'd never talked before! And, oh, I don't know, it was just such a revelation to me, that a man could be so . . . gentle.'

I'd nod. 'Yeah. He's an old softie sometimes.' And we'd grin, knowing we'd never have said such a thing in his company.

My father was always banned by my mother from our 'quiet times'. If he came in, habitual coffee cup in hand, hunting us down to ask about dinner, she'd say, 'We're just having a quiet time together, dear,' and he'd leave the room again with a startled look, just as he did when he walked in on me once in the bathroom. Instead of squealing, like my sister Lucy did if anyone so much as rattled the handle, I'd slipped under the water I'd laughed so hard. Poor regional-manager Dad had looked like a dog with a bee-stung nose.

My mother would continue her stories about men, about love and, obliquely, sex (the two were always linked), and I'd take them in with an acutely phonetic memory: all her inflections and emphases stored up for replay to Jenny when she visited next time. Then we'd compare what my mother had said with what we read in magazines, working out our own balance between dubious dismissal and wholesale belief.

I remember one of those magazine items in particular. We were fifteen, and Jenny and I had decided to risk going back to her place after school. The *Cleo* magazine we'd bought was safely tucked into my bag. In it was a 'sealed section' on women's bodies. We had already read it side by side in a coffee bar, the pages spread out on our laps, so that the table top concealed them from passers-by. We'd pored over the diagrams of the perfectly intricate, interlocking structure of the female organs: the tubes and ovaries looked to me like the long, curved stems and full buds of tropical flowers about to bloom, the glands and collecting ducts of the breast like filigreed trees, clustered intimately together. It was difficult to imagine all this lush botany going on inside our bodies, to map such bustling yet two-dimensional sketches beneath the curves and mounds that our school uniforms did their best to conceal.

We read the cut section seriously, silently, heads bent with such concentration that the man at the coffee bar counter leaned over the serving top, dishcloth in one hand, and called out good-humouredly, 'Hey! You two think this is a church? Y'll turn away my customers!' We joked with him, but after calling attention to ourselves decided to pack up and leave.

Back in Jen's room, she rolled a mug of hot chocolate slowly between her palms, as if she were shaping clay.

'You know some of those things that article talked about?' she asked, a small frown complicating the smooth skin of her forehead.

'What things?'

'You know—about how sex feels and things.'

'Yeah . . .'

'Do you know where it is?'

The steam from my mug caught in my lungs and I coughed.

'What—you mean, the vagina?'

Jenny frowned more deeply. 'No, Marie. That's obvious. But I mean—you know.'

It had puzzled me as well. In none of those talks with my mother had she mentioned pleasure. Apart from the one or two stories about how she'd met my father, it was all mechanics and facts: cramps, swelling, headaches, moodswings, and warnings about how simple it was to get pregnant: 'As easy as fish grow fins.' But our *Cleo* magazine talked about orgasm. There were two pages of anonymous readers' replies about this new word: some people saying they'd never had it; other people asking if what they described might be one; others bursting out of the columns with their exclamation marks. One even mentioned multiple orgasms, which sounded like an illness. The arrows on the diagrams pointed to a place that I just didn't think could be right. I admitted to Jenny that I didn't know. She didn't seem surprised, but said, setting down her mug of hot chocolate,

'We'd better work it out.'

Jenny slipped the magazine out of my bag, flicking it open to the sealed section and the fine-line, black and white diagrams of the female body. She turned on her transistor radio so that we could talk underneath the music.

'"Ignorance is dangerous,"' she said, reading from the article. '"It is important for our health that we learn as much as possible about our own bodies and the way they work. Most of us can feel uncomfortable asking parents or teachers about more private aspects of ourselves, such as the nature of the menstrual cycle."'

Jenny flipped a page. '"But it is possible for us to educate ourselves. The first thing is for us to learn about how all parts of our bodies look, as well as how they feel when touched. You should use a mirror for this step."'

Jenny bounded up again and went to her dressing table where she kept a hand mirror. Steadying herself with one hand on the dresser, she kicked off her shoes and started to pull off her tights.

'Jenny!'

I was used to her joking way of trying to catch me unaware in a way I'd almost become addicted to: the way her daring impelled me out of my shyness, like a learner parachutist encouraged to jump. Occasionally, she pushed too far: like the time I watched for her while she shoplifted a pair of black tights as sheer, glistening and slick as oil. The way she told me what she was going to do, but then just slipped off without allowing me a chance to refuse had at first filled me with a vicious sense of betrayal. Ironically, it made me a sharp lookout. And although I was furious with her afterwards, the relief sung through my veins like that first illicit drink of Stone's green ginger wine we'd shared in the park with her brothers.

Now she had really unnerved me. She had moved the low stool that fitted underneath her dressing table closer to the centre of the room.

'What's the matter, Marie? Your mother's a nurse!'

In my head, I accepted what the magazine said about exploring—but in my skin, I was already crippled with misery and modesty. I hated undressing in front of anyone, even Jenny. At school, at gym or swimming, I was one of those who had worked out various Houdini ways of slipping off my bra while still wearing my shirt, and getting clothes on underneath a damp towel. There was a breed of girls, like Jenny, who hardly seemed to know the difference between their bodies clothed and their bodies exposed—they carried on conversations, face to face, shifting their weight from leg to leg, raising their arms and letting them fall, just as they would fully dressed. I caught their actions only in the most troubled of sideways glances, my face, sweaty from the exertions of PE, quickly lowered again as I lumbered back into my own uniform. I felt as graceless as a fat pigeon struggling for balance on an ill-chosen twig.

Joss, who has seen photos of me as a teenager, draws me to him whenever I recount these episodes. He kisses my neck, and laughs, 'Where did you get these ideas? Where?' But I loathed my body then: had stood in front of my mirror at home taking fistfuls of the flesh on my thighs and at my waist, pinching and twisting it until tears sprang up. Then, the blotchiness of my face and my swollen eyes convinced my mother that I wasn't well and she allowed me to be excused from the family meal. My father, who had always been thin and wiry, could only make misdirected attempts to cheer me up. 'Extra fat supply's good for survival,' he'd boom. You'll outlive us all when the Big Quake comes!' I'd burst into tears again and withdraw to my bed, nursing my hunger like a hatred.

Jenny dropped the hand holding her mirror to her side. 'You can turn away,' she said. 'I'm not making you watch. But you should do it too.'

'This is *juvenile*,' I shot at her, but wondered if actually it was me being a terrible prude. I turned my back.

Jenny was quiet.

'You act like it's a bloody DIY furniture kit,' I muttered, filtering my discomfort through a sarcastic sharpness. 'Sometimes you're a weird bitch.'

I waited and waited for her to say something. Then a door slammed, and I heard footsteps coming down the corridor. They stopped at Jenny's room, and the door handle rattled.

'Are you girls in there?'

It was Marion. I turned and saw Jenny pulling on her tights as rapidly as she could. I slipped over and hid the magazine in my bag, then went over to open the door, willing, willing the expression on my face to relax into the most convincing blank I could counterfeit.

Marion looked surprisingly unthreatening—her eyes were sleepy with drink, and one of her pupils had dilated dramatically. I remember thinking it might have been a sign that she was about to black out. It made her seem lopsided and vague.

'If you're here for dinner,' she said, 'you're not.' She rocked a little and put her hand on the doorpost. I could smell her breath, still sweet from wine, but I knew that in the morning something decayed would press me back if I stood this close.

When I had first noticed that scent of something on the turn, it had seemed so obvious that I thought, perhaps, sweat had made her perfume curdle. But as I encountered it more often, I learned that it was the just-woken, sour-sheets smell of a heavy drinker. I asked my mother once why someone might be an alcoholic, trying to sound off-hand, saying, 'Oh, you know, it's just this book I'm reading . . .' She must have guessed who I meant, but she answered me frankly, and just as casually: 'Well, there are people who think it might be hereditary, or at least biochemical. But then, there might be other people who aren't affected by those things. Maybe they've become terribly unhappy, so they drink to blunt things down, to go numb.' I absorbed all this, but it was one topic I never knew how to broach with Jenny. I was always waiting for her to bring it up first, for her to crack some smarmy comment about Marion being smashed, half-cut, pissed-as-a-fart, arse-faced as usual. But Jen hadn't openly discussed the drinking since Christmas when Marion had shattered the perfume bottle. It made me feel the subject was too intimate for Jenny, was almost taboo—and, after I had learned to recognise the oniony breath, I was oddly reminded of someone else. A memory that came up every time I shifted myself a little when Marion came close.

Her name was Catherine. She was a girl at my school, a little older than me, perhaps seven or eight. (She too has disappeared: after she runs into the crowd, she runs into nothingness. It's as if she dissolves into the white edges around a film screen that still shows crowded streets. What happens to all those names that people the past?) She was thin, energetic, and at every lunch break wrapped the hem of her tartan skirt around the gym bars in the playground to protect her palms from burning as she spun round and round, round and round, her brown plait whipping in the air like a jump-rope. All I really knew about Catherine was that she played on the bars: at six years old, that was what mattered. She wore the same orange, hand-knitted cardigan every day, the same fawn and white plaid skirt—and that was Catherine. It was how you knew her.

One day, other kids I didn't know were grouped near the bars. Someone sang out her name, up and down, through several notes on a scale, long and dizzying, and the thing had started. They were after her.

Why don't you change your clothes, don't you have any clothes, why don't you wash, don't you ever have a wash, are you really poor, too poor to have a wash, you're poor, you're poor, you're poor, poor, poor?

Catherine still spun and spun, perhaps trying to spin them away like thread, to spool them up and loop them right out of her hearing. But as she reached the top of one turn, someone yanked up the back of her skirt and she was held there—tail in the air, her head centimetres from the ground, her face filling red with blood. She couldn't wheel on, or her skirt would rip. *Look! Look! Look! She doesn't wipe her bum!* Her underwear, snowdrop white and printed with blue bows, was smudged with a small brown stain.

The kids were stunned. Then wild. Victorious. *Catherine stinks! Catherine stinks! Catherine stinks!* Having won, they could let her go, but let her loose like a cat with a shoe still tied to its tail. Her skirt was released, and I expected her to explain. I knew it must have been an accident; their discovery had been a fluke. But Catherine lowered herself to the ground, her expression still struggling to pretend deafness—and then she ran. The playground seemed vast: I lost sight of her amongst all the different, milling games. A taste, sick and milky, came into my mouth. Now the kids would come for me, lift my home-made, hand-me-down, box-cut dress. But they moved separately and effortlessly away, quick and scudding as the ducks that scooted along the creek beside our school.

I never let myself mention the reek of alcohol on Marion to Jenny. Memory prevented me, as if my childhood self were saying, *You mustn't hurt her. What do you know about anything? It's private, you've got no right.* And by then, Jenny wouldn't admit that Marion might be unhappy. Whenever Marion leaned near me, I would move away as discreetly as possible, cautiously yet almost instinctively moderating my response to her.

That night, as she steadied herself against the doorframe, I censored myself as always. 'Are you all right, Marion?' I held out a hand to help her to balance.

'I'm not bloody well cooking. You can fix your own dinner, you two.' And then, as if one side of her brain had cut lines with the other, she took a ten-dollar note from her pocket, crumpled it up and threw it into the bedroom, delivering the rest of her punishment as she gave a small grunt of physical effort. 'And you can bloody go and buy it as well.' She made her way towards the double bedroom, leaning her weight now and then on her palms against the corridor wall.

I turned back to look behind me into Jenny's room. She was uncrumpling the ten dollars.

'Close call,' I said to her, hoping she could hear that I was sorry for my earlier sarcasm. She pocketed the money, her eyes giving me their characteristic assessment.

'Nope,' she said, and formed a pursed-lip smile, as if keeping something back. 'Think I found it.' She lifted her coat from the back of her door. 'Hamburgers or fish and chips?'

I lay in bed that night, hands perched on my stomach for what seemed like hours before I could touch myself. My ears almost hurt from the effort of listening for one of my parents approaching down the hallway. I thought about my sisters, and how, like Mum, they had never talked to me about what the *Cleo* magazine had said. How Jenny was the only one who'd asked such questions. I imagined my sisters together, whispering about these things after one of their double dates. I thought of the way they always moved apart when I came into the kitchen while they were talking. One would rinse cups; one would look out the window and sigh, running her hands down her ribs, smoothing her shirt. As if my arrival were a reminder of something they didn't want to think about. I was the kid, the swot: all the things they wanted to get away from. From being girls instead of women. I wondered if they'd always known about the sort of information I'd found in *Cleo*. And why nobody had ever told me before.

In the safety of my own room, I'd looked closely at the magazine again, and in the locked bathroom examined myself in a hand mirror. Startled, I'd dressed again hurriedly. Now I persisted with what the magazine and Jenny said was so important. But I didn't feel any warm tingling: just that my hands were cold. I still didn't know what all the exclamation marks or Jenny's odd smile were about. I decided I couldn't have developed enough, despite my height.

Two memories strike me equally from after the time we'd read the *Cleo*. First there's one night down at the beach. (I know I've told Joss about that night, but there is a compulsion to search for new detail, by going over and over these events, as if I could no more stop myself from recounting them than I could stop them returning to mind . . .) And then there is the meeting with Russell and Blake, at the night club, when it all... but I must try to separate each evening out, go more slowly, try to find out why. If only *why* could be clear, solid, tangible. If only I could come across it with the satisfied outcry of someone searching for and finding a lost locket in the sand, an engraved silver oval, shining like a tiny pool of water. Slip it into your palm, ease the hinged wings open with a fingernail and there, inside, there it would be. But it's not that easy. It's not that easy, even with Joss listening, lending another perspective.

First of all, the beach. The stretch which we usually wandered along was about half an hour's walk, or a fifteen-minute bus-ride, from my place. You could see for miles along the rocks and sand, and that helped to make it seem isolated from the town. We'd always been warned about the unpredictable rip-tides and the surge: only a small section was deemed safe for swimming in summer. If I turned my back to the coastal road and listened to the breakers, it would feel as if we'd left everything behind. Perhaps it was because the beach road eventually became the highway out of town, and because occasionally, on the horizon, we'd see huge ships—tankers and liners that slipped past like low whispers, saying, Look at the world beyond yourselves. Their steady motion gave me the same entranced sensation as gazing down at the water that raced below a moving deck.

We had stayed on at the beach late one weekend spring evening; Jonathon and Gareth had shared swigs of a miniature bottle of Jack Daniels with us before mooching off to hang out with friends who could borrow their family cars. I'd grown to enjoy their easy-going humour and its equally easy inclusion of me, and I half wanted them to stay. Didn't want nightfall to come. In the end, Jenny and I decided to linger there alone, as if we could draw out the light a little longer simply by not conceding to go inside.

Jenny was in a stupid mood—jumping from rock to rock too quickly, stumbling sometimes, twisting her ankle once, but just giggling helplessly, staggering up and running to the short stretch of shingle before the sand, where she spun, arms out. It wasn't that she'd had too much to drink; neither of us much liked 'whisky burn', as she called it, holding her throat. I can't explain what happened that night with alcohol. It was just the way she was sometimes.

I tried to catch up with her, picking my way more carefully, singing out ('Jenny, Jenny, Jenny Wren') before we started half-heartedly throwing wet sand at each other down near the tideline, then collapsed, looking out to sea.

We were quiet there for a while. I'd always loved those times when Jen and I just sat, at rest in each other's silence. I watched the waves, and drifted off into thinking about where we would be in a year's time—five years'—ten. I wanted a job that would send me overseas—and saw myself striding across a courtyard somewhere, meeting Jen at a café table, laughing, in sunlight. Already I couldn't imagine us separated. She was always there, alongside me, when I visualised myself elsewhere. Subconsciously, I must have known she was my catalyst. Together we'd escape the town's flat, grey, sheltering sky, and the suburban sameness of the streets which threatened to work on us like a vice, moulding us into one of my aunts, my sisters or, worse, Marion. Someone who'd never insisted on the justice of dreaming themselves into another life.

As I watched a wave collect, I held my breath at a sudden rise of excitement.

I turned to Jenny.

'Jen, where do you think we'll be in ten years?'

It was a game we'd played before, addictive in its thrilling paradox of hope and doubt, for the way it intensified things, outlined the immediate scene before us more vividly. We had to be careful how we answered. Our responses could work like breath blown over dice for luck before they were rolled. As if anything we said could change our whole course.

Jenny gave a shiver, and clasped her arms around her knees, where she leaned her chin. 'Ten years,' she said, as if it were the first time one of us had asked the question. 'Ten years.' She lifted her chin again, watching the waves. 'Okay.' She smiled. 'I'll be living in Paris, doing—I don't know—translation for an embassy. Yeah. And exactly ten years from this very evening, I'll be at a cocktail party, where people from Zaire and Algeria and America and South America and everywhere will kiss my hand and compliment me on my exquisite French. And Spanish. And Portuguese, too.'

'And then you'll introduce them to me.'

'Exactly. You'll have to be in Paris for an international academic symposium on the role of sociology in . . . in . . .'

'Urban planning,' I hazarded.

'Do they go together?'

'No idea.'

'Oh well, sounds flash. So, anyway, you'll walk in, looking drop-dead gorgeous, wearing . . . wearing a dress with a deep V cut into the back which is trimmed with shiny, eight-sided jet beads, and I'll say, "This is my oldest and dearest friend, Marie Conway . . ."'

'Yeah, I'll have just flown in to Paris from London, where I'm based for most of the year—the rest in New York.'

'Where you have a penthouse.'

'Where I have a penthouse and—a kitchen with barstools.'

'And a spare room for me, when I have to fly in to the States.' She leaned against me for a moment.

'Which will be often, so we'll see each other at least once a month.'

'Yeah, and we'll be on the phone to each other the rest of the time.'

'Usually while we're having champagne in our bubble baths.'

Jenny laughed, and lay back again, propping herself up on her elbows. Gradually, her attention drew away and focused inwards.

I watched a slight breeze lift her hair and trail a curl across her vision. She brushed it aside, and I looked back out to sea, thinking of how, when I'd escaped, I would write back home to my parents. I imagined them still living in our little road, cupped close, protected from the world—the world out there. I wondered how they could want to live in a street like that for ever. Same driveway, same walls, same old neighbours, same old boredom.

I didn't think, at the time, that the boredom was purely mine, and purely selfish. How privileged I was, with all the material comforts I took for granted and which they worked so hard to give us. I didn't consider what demands their careers must have made, or what it was like for them having to ride the rollercoaster of my and my sisters' adolescence. And I'd forgotten how unsettled I'd been when we first moved to that town. Already, it was the 'same bloody' town, with the hamster-wheel of school, study, school, study. A bedroom where I knew every inch of the carpet, every watermark on the ceiling, where nothing seemed to change. The four dead walls of compressed study time—those, ironically, were the source of my first real aspiration: to get to university. Life would be different there.

I stared at the waves, which rippled in from the horizon like a bolt of flourished satin. 'You know, I told Dad my latest history mark last night,' I said to Jen.

'Yeah? Was he pleased?'

I dug the toes of my sneakers as far as I could into the sand. 'I don't know. Sort of. I suppose so. It's kind of hard to tell. He said it was good, but then he said'—I imitated him—'"Never really liked history. Depressing subject. All those mistakes lined up, one after the other—all those wars and battles—hated essay-writing, too. How are your maths and economics coming along?" It's like he thinks he's grooming me to be one of his branch accountants, though I don't know how many times I've told him I'm leaving for university and am not going to work for him. It's just not what I want.' I stared at the sand I'd scuffed up.

'But he did say it was a good mark.'

I unburied my shoes, then began digging them in all over again. 'Yeah, in a way.'

She frowned at me then. 'You know you're good. That should be enough. And he can't *make* you work for him. What's he going to do, chain you to him? He might *want* you to stay here, but Marie, your Dad—if going away is what you want, he'll be supportive. In the end, he just wants you to be happy, don't you think?'

I stared at my shoes and gave a half-hearted nod.

'Well, anyway,' she said, in a finalising tone, 'I'd rather have your family any day. I think you're lucky. Really lucky.'

I gazed out at the white strands which had begun to lace the waves, thinking this over: feeling guilty for complaining, but also relieved, grateful for the way Jenny's view lightened and lifted me out of my sense of enclosure. I wanted a way to articulate it to her, to say what she meant to me. But the harder I thought, the thicker and slower the words came.

Then, unexpectedly, she sat up, and started to scan the beach. She stood. She turned around and around on the spot, her arms wide, embracing it all—crucified upon it all. She kicked a spray of sand into the air, and called out, over the waves and against the high-pitched peals from the waltzing gulls, *'Why doesn't someone just take us away?'* Then she let her arms drop, and she spun again.

'Fuck, I'm restless,' she said. 'Let's go.'

By the time we had scrambled up on to the road again it had started to rain, very slightly. We were wearing only light cotton jerseys and jeans, and stood at the bus shelter hugging our arms to ourselves. The faded timetable said that the next bus wouldn't be for twenty minutes, and Jen kept stamping her feet with her repeated, 'Come on, come on!'

It made the waiting worse—I was quite happy to let my thoughts slip into the rain, to stand there quietly, smelling the sand and the asphalt weave together their soaked scents, and feeling the light drops mist over my face. If I concentrated on small discomforts in the right way—if I gave myself up to them—it was a kind of escape in itself. A meditation, I suppose. But Jenny kept stomping and fidgeting on the spot, niggling me back to reality.

Finally, in the distance, we heard an engine and I began to search my pockets for the busfare. But what came into view was a big, black beaten-up car, its belly low to the ground. I felt a reluctant *thud* in my stomach, and stepped back to stay protected by the bus shelter.

With a shout and a wave, Jen stepped into the road.

'Jen!'

Disbelieving and annoyed, I wanted to drag her back. But the driver was already pulling over, and as the car drew up, he cranked down a window. I scouted quickly in the direction our bus would come, then warily watched the driver lean over and open the passenger door.

'Gidday,' he said. 'What are you girls doing out here?'

'Trying to leave,' Jenny said, her voice sounding falsely sweet. My heart flickered on and off like a badly wired light, but she shot me a glance that said, *Look at him, Marie!*

I judged the driver through the opened car door. He wore blue cotton overalls and a brown leather jacket. On his knuckles, which I could see as he gripped the door frame, there were small greenish crosses; he also had two small blue dots tattooed on one cheekbone. His hair was long, curly, blond. The car ashtray was choked with cigarette butts, as if he chain-smoked, and the closeness of his facial bones to the surface of his skin seemed related to this. I imagined an energy burning in him, wasting his body away, whittling him down to the thin structure of his skeleton. Looking at him, I had a sudden image of my father's hand raised and slamming down on a table. *'Loser! Drop-out!'* The picture of my usually placid father's vehemence jarred me into looking at Jenny again for reassurance.

And, as she stood there, hands in her pockets, giving a theatrical little shiver and hop on the spot, I knew exactly what Jenny was going to do. I reached out for her arm again, warning, 'Jen—' but she took her hands from her pockets and rested one on the open car door.

'It's pretty freezing,' she said. 'You heading into town?'

He grinned, his teeth cigarette-butt yellow, sharp and strangely regular, like a saw. 'Yehp. Can I give you a lift?'

His voice was even, and he looked as if he were running a finger over her, top to bottom, testing her finish, her gloss. Instinctive dislike mounted inside me, but I tried not to let it alter my expression. He wouldn't have noticed, anyway. His gaze trailed back up to Jenny's face, and instead of recoiling, as I'd hoped she might, she seemed drawn in. I don't suppose it would have mattered to Jen who he was at that point. He was someone. Anyone. And she was sixteen: full and ripe as honeycomb.

She swung her hair over her shoulders, and moved her weight to one side, edging up one hip slightly. 'That'd be great,' she answered.

'Jen,' I countered, 'I'd rather wait.'

'Hey, it's okay,' the man said, moving farther into the car and stretching his arm along the back of the passenger seat. 'Jump in. No problem.'

I found my gaze straying over his face again, fascinated despite myself. I realised one of his eyes was blue, one brown—wasn't that like David Bowie?—and when he smiled there were deep, attractive lines beside his mouth, etched as if with a sharp tool. He must have been thirty—no, thirty five. *Christ*, what was I—what was Jenny thinking? I tugged on her arm again.

'Come on, Jen.' She slipped free, with a smooth twist of her arm, and gave one of her half-octave, climbing laughs. 'Look, I think we should wait for the bus.'

The driver seemed amused, but appeared too to be holding something aside. He leaned over slightly, and shifted four beer cans from a six-pack from the empty seat to the floor. 'Plenty of room,' he said.

Irritated, I moved between Jenny and the car, turning slightly so he wouldn't hear me. I wanted to grind the words into her like nails. 'Jen, don't be stupid.'

She paused for a split second, but then she said, 'God, you're difficult, Marie. What are you so afraid of? Let's just get a lift home.'

'No, Jen, I don't *want* to.' I knew I sounded whinging and petulant. Jenny gave me a blunt look of frustration, and embarrassment. Then her face dropped into a secretive blank. 'I know what I'm doing, Marie,' she said. 'You don't have to look after me.'

The back of my neck prickled. The guy gunned his engine, and Jenny bobbed down, not even asking me to get in with her. She passed him a quick 'Sorry about that!', before she curved herself into the car, as if she were zipping something close to her skin. The driver kept his arm stretched out along the back of her seat, and swung away from the bus shelter, steering one-handed. Jenny didn't turn and wave.

A small, furious pincer of tears clenched and twisted in my throat. 'You stupid, stupid shit! You stupid bloody *shit!*' I wanted to hit something, kick free of myself—and Jenny: get rid of it all, like dirt scuffed from a boot-side.

I looked around me: now the beach was threateningly desolate, the road a route for some coming menace. Maybe it really would have been safer if I had climbed in with her. Then I thought again of the way the man's eyes had seemed to finger Jenny, as if the sight of her were silk. I saw his arm stretched out across the back of her seat still, and all the tension in that scene was suddenly released, a whipcord sapling branch flung back into my face. I heard her again. 'I know what I'm doing, Marie. You don't have to look after me.' There was something more than recklessness in the timbre of her voice, something level. Straight and calculated. As if, should risk come into it, she'd only move closer, to amplify its hiss and static.

Why couldn't I express these misgivings to Jenny then? Why did I treat so many of my own reactions as a kind of awkward innocence instead of a strength of instinct? So often back then, I simply felt naïve. Now I think that naïveté was a form of prescience. Self-preservation: a sense of myself, of my limits, which I didn't need to test through experience. Is that what finally kept me safe? And how do I reconcile that with the fact that so many of the experiences we lived through together have shaped me?

That night, I felt so stranded, so abandoned, I was momentarily surprised by the bus headlights in the distance. Desperately, I waved it down, and as it slowed beside me I scrabbled at the door with both hands, trying to hurry it open. The driver turned in his seat as I jumped up the steps.

'All right there, love?' I fumbled for some change.

'Yeah,' I said. But my fingers seemed unable to separate out one coin from another.

'Never mind,' he said, and took a quick look in the rear-view mirror, checking the one or two passengers on board. He waved me down the aisle, and I sank into a seat, feeling my temples drumming with delayed relief that I was safe, on a bus, going home. I leaned my head against the window, looking out at the last view of the sea before we turned uphill.

I know what I'm doing, Marie. You don't have to look after me.

I closed my eyes, and clenched my hands in my pockets until a small pain burnt deep in the joints.

The next day was a Saturday, I'm sure of that, because I know I had to wait until after 10 in the morning, before I could escape Mum's housework routine. I cycled over to Jen's, standing up all the way to pump at my pedals until it felt my legs would collapse under the effort.

I let my bicycle clatter to the ground outside the front steps, and ran up to lean on the doorbell, long and steady. Marion answered. The skin beneath her eyes was sunken and dark. She dropped her shoulders in tired irritation when she saw it was me. Without opening the door farther, she called for Jenny, then stalked off, her body with that horrible intent you see in some mothers in the street, or in a park. When you know, with a paralysing mixture of foresight and disbelief, that a toddler is about to be screamed at, or shaken, or snatched up too roughly. I stepped up quickly to the threshold, and watched Marion aim for Jenny's room. She shook the door in its socket and demanded,

'Get the bell, will you?'

I didn't hear a reply, but Marion gave up, exasperated, and disappeared off down the hallway. I closed the front door, and went over to tap at Jen's.

'Jenny? It's me.'

When the door clicked open, her room was still dim, and she was tying her bathrobe.

'Hello, you,' she said, smiling sleepily.

Half wanting to hug her for being unbroken, half wanting to put both hands against her shoulders and shove, I did neither—but marched over to her curtains. I swept them apart, taking a narrow satisfaction in her small, light-sensitive cry. She flopped onto her bed and lay down again, one arm over her eyes.

'Talk to me,' I said to her, still standing.

I saw her chest rise and fall with an exaggerated sigh.

I went and stood over her. 'Talk to me,' I said again.

Then I noticed. Her neck and below her collar bone were bare now that her long hair had fallen back to the pillow.

Two little strawberry stains. Like new birth marks. I moved closer. Crushed, sucked cherry shapes. I knew the rush and sting she would have felt through them. And how he would have known the salty, sesame taste of a girl's skin. How those petal shapes would be tender to touch now, and would change to brown and yellow, like a bruised windfall apple, or damaged camellias. But with a kind of humiliation, I knew this only from those times when, as kids, schoolmates and I had played at giving ourselves love bites, on our own knees, on our own arms. With an illogical crumbling of emotions, I felt gauche, backwards, betrayed, abandoned, mean—and—could it be covetous? Wanting Jenny's experience, even as I censured her for it? I bent down, and pressed my thumb to the hickey near her collar bone. She slapped my hand away.

'Don't.'

'What happened?'

'Nothing.'

'It wasn't bloody nothing. You left me there . . .'

'You're all right, aren't you?'

'*You* mightn't have been. What the hell did you think you were doing? You don't just get into some strange guy's car like that . . .'

She lifted herself up on one elbow, interrupting me. 'Look. He drove me back to town, he asked me to share a can of beer, and then we just fooled around a bit.' She opened her arms, as she had on the beach, and craned her neck at an angle. 'See?' she said, unnecessarily, which she knew. 'That's it. I told you I knew what I was doing. Why don't you *relax*, Marie? It's not like you can get pregnant if you just ride in someone's car.'

Again I wanted to shove her.

She shrugged. 'Anyway, it turns out Dale knows the Barrys from down the road. He says he hangs out at their garage sometimes. He says he thought he recognised me.'

I couldn't believe she thought knowing the Barry brothers was some kind of recommendation. It was Jenny herself who'd told me the rumours about the Barrys and their mates. The Barrys, their gang, and girls in the pines. The Barrys and girls on the beach. The Barrys taking turns with their dates in the back of cars: one girl coming home crying, and her father going round with a cricket bat, grabbing a can of petrol from the Barrys' workshop and threatening to set the whole place on fire.

'Oh great, so he's a friend of *theirs*?' I gave her a filthy look.

She sat up, and swung her legs over the bed. 'God, let's just drop it. Marion's already had a go at me for being late last night. I don't need you bitching as well.'

I wanted to back away. In my head, I heard what I should have said. *'Why are you my friend.'* It wouldn't have been asking a question. Not really. It would have been stating it, saying that the previous night had, for the first time, set up the possibility of opposition between us. *'Why do we even bother being friends. Why stay with me if you're going to treat me like this, if you think you're so sophisticated. Is there anything about me that's worth your trouble.'* The words lined up in my mind, expressionless as exercises chalked up on a blackboard. They should have been rankling, passionate, an argument. But I was drained and numb. The most intense feeling I had at that point was a floating, surreal uncertainty. As if I levitated outside us both, and watched us on a spot-lit, elevated stage. We'd been through so much together—I remembered that feeling of complete closeness I'd felt on the beach—but now, I thought, Why us? How different we were, when we first met. Was it really just circumstance—my need, her curiosity, my loneliness, her hunger for any ally—that had pulled us together and held us for this long? What was I doing here, standing in her bedroom, when she'd made it so clear that she'd separated herself from me last night?

My long, staring silence discomfited Jenny. She turned away from me. 'It's all over now, anyway. We're both here, aren't we?' There was an off-key note, a string hit amiss, as she went to her wardrobe and rifled through her clothes. I didn't answer, and she confronted me, dropping her hands, her brow in an upwards furrow.

'Marie?'

Answering would have meant cracking through the thin layer of ice that had formed over my lips.

She took a step towards me, her arms out a little. 'Please, Marie. Don't be like this. It was nothing. It was just for a bit of fun, just to *do* something, do you know what I mean? To have something happen for once.' She paused. 'Have someone notice me.'

It seemed to shift once more as she stood there, pleading. It was ridiculous that we could be on the verge of an argument. Me and Jenny. JennyandMarie. The frost in my throat softened, and I weakened, dismissing it all, embarrassed for other reasons now: for seeming so uptight, so intense. Jenny turned back to her wardrobe, her entire posture changed with the release of that magnetic repulsion between us.

'Do you want a coffee?' she said.

There were many small signals that morning which told me she felt an element of guilt about the way she'd left me the night before. Or uncertainty, even, about the impulse that had made her step out into the road, into the rain, into Dale's car . . . Her glance kept flitting to the side, as she meshed her fingers together until the knuckles were blanched: unmeshed, then meshed them again. I began to get the feeling that she hadn't enjoyed her escapade that much. Her indifferent responses would lightly touch my questions away as if they were small, moving beads of mercury, and irrelevant. I lost the confidence to ask her anything else, and the topic itself grew so weirdly amorphous and elusive that I quietly internalised the questions, leaving them to gather.

Even so, now that Jenny knew that Dale was a friend of the Barrys, I expected her to choose the route past their garage whenever we went to and from town. And on the first few occasions when walking that way was unavoidable, Jenny did straighten her spine as we drew near, walking as if she were carrying something breakable. One afternoon, Dale was there, and she waited on the footpath, calling out, 'Hi there, you!' Dale glanced at the Barrys, then gave her the same slow 'Gidday' that they had. He flicked a blue rag over his knuckles, then went back to his car. Jenny's face grew blotched with restrained feeling, and she walked quickly away. Until the next time—when, if she saw Dale there, some wish to establish that her experience had mattered, that she was an exception to the girls rumoured about in connection with the Barrys, must have made her stop, say hi, and linger in his sightline.

Dale's lack of interest meant that soon Jenny avoided the route past the Barrys' garage. It was as if she'd conceded to herself that an experiment had failed. But there was one more incident, when we saw Dale some months after that—I'm not sure how long: again he seemed to set up hope, only to send it skittling over and spinning on its side. Jenny and I were walking through town when a horn sounded—one of the yodelling, exhibitionist kinds. Jenny turned, and saw who it was. Caught off guard, she stepped towards the kerb to speak to him. Dale had dropped his speed down to a crawl, and lifted his palm. It was the simplest of gestures that still grew cryptic, because he drove away, the car windows turning opaque as he circled into the dusk.

Jenny dropped down off the pavement and crossed over to the other side of the road to walk down another street—not in the direction we'd been heading—distracted, or perhaps covering for her movements.

I sped up a little. 'Are you okay?'

Her eyelids fluttered, in the look of someone whose concentration has just been broken. A difficult surfacing.

'Are you all right?'

'Yeah, I'm fine. Where are we going?'

I watched her, perplexed. 'That way.' I pointed.

'Right. Let's do that.'

We doubled back, Jenny pulling her denim jacket closely to her, holding her collar against some unexpected inner chill. She shivered, then refocused.

'What shall we do, what shall we do?' she said, hopping, half-pirouetting, then taking my own collar briefly, leaning in to me so that I could feel her warm breath. 'I want something to happen, to really *happen!*' Then she was off, running, and I caught her excitement and ran with her—into some scene, some night that I've lost.

I glance at the kitchen clock, the small of my back sore from crouching in my chair. I've been inclined sharply forward, as if to hold voices in close to me: voices filtering through the darkness, under the window cracks, up from the street.

I can feel it all again with a tightness in my chest, as if there is a hand under my heart that lifts and clenches. The unpredictability of Jenny. Sometimes, the unfairness of it: the cruelty, even. But also the euphoria, the seductive high, the attraction. How rarely I feel that giddiness now . . .

Is that it? Is that why thinking I saw her today has shaken me so much? Does she, in some way, mean certain qualities that I have lost? So that I'm thrown less because I thought it was really Jenny, than because thinking I could see deepened lines and changes to her face was a realisation of how much time has passed? How I've aged, but how some questions, some needs, still hurt? Would I be proud to meet her again? What could I show her of my life? Does she, what would she, think of me now?

Sometimes, I'm still not sure if I did the right thing by Jenny. Or even if I'm doing the right thing now. Already in my thirties, finally concentrating again on my training, but with Joss sometimes whispering to me in the night, one hand cupping my breast, the edge of his thumb knuckle gently stroking a nipple as his mouth brushes my ear: 'Do you think, one day, we might have children?' And the confusion his question brings: No, no, I'm not ready yet, I hardly know who I am, I've hardly proven I can do any of the things I've always said I would do . . . And then, however many days after Joss's caressing, his gentle, understated confession and my silent resistance, I'll find myself gazing at a toddler in the supermarket or on the swings at the park. I'll share a smile with the mother or father, as if we have an instant understanding.

Could I talk to Jenny about these feelings? Or would it be too painful for her? Too painful for her still?

Yet it was always in the nature of our friendship that fractures were healed over, forgotten, in the thick of just being together—as happened over Dale. It always built and rebuilt, like the game of hand over hand, palm arching knuckles, the small clasped tower always the same height, same strength, same dimensions. Hand on hand.

So that when we met Russell and Blake, it was as if there had never been any jealousy and hurt between us before. Now I think of that meeting as the first point—the point to which all of the things that went wrong can be traced. But that's not fair; Russell had no idea. Not one of us did.

So many memories seem to want my attention, pulling and softly whispering at me, not to be left out. As if, should I run through them all, tending and examining, they would obediently fall into line—event behind event, an orderly, manageable, single-file. Yet it couldn't ever be so: the details of months and months of my time with Jenny have achromatised, like the real pigment in paintings: aged into something far from the original.

Joss has been very patient. After a long night talking and drinking red wine which we've mulled with a tiny mob cap of spices, my memories have meandered, contradicted, triggered each other like the games of random word association my sisters used to play on long car journeys when we were small. Now Joss is tired, and he hugs me in a way that tells me he needs to get some sleep.

He frowns a little, unsure whether he should leave me yet.

'You know, you'll probably never see her again—this woman on the train, I mean. Whether or not it was Jenny.' He pauses. 'I think you'll have to make yourself forget her. As much as you can. At least, you'll just have to forget today.' His palms go up in a gesture which says the situation is beyond him, a rope that has run through his hands.

I hug him, tell him I'm not sleepy yet, but that he can go off to bed. I say I'll probably read, perhaps catch up on letters to family in New Zealand until I'm drowsy. He moves off to the hallway, his expression clearing, as if even now he's submitting to the peaceful wash of sleep.

I take out the stationery set that I reserve for writing letters home. I don't write often, but when I do, I immerse myself in it completely. I take pleasure in buying a paper design that suits my parents' tastes, and I usually make myself a pot of tea, as if they're in my kitchen and we're talking things over. I can understand them more, now that I'm older. Each time Joss asks me about children, I realise how hard I was on my parents, how inadequate I would be trying to do their job! But I don't write to my sisters. Whenever I imagine them at the other end of my anecdotes, I gum up. The life I've made for myself is so separate from theirs. I picture them in their homes, which are always having some part of them renovated, though everything else is as neat as index cards in an alphabetised box—Heather's in autumnal colours, Lucy's in spring pinks that to me look medicinal—and I'm instantly bored. I know that to them I'm just as incomprehensible: they seem to think that because I'm overseas, I'm still 'just travelling', in other words, that I'm perpetually running away, even though I have a flat, a job, a partner and a part-time course to attend . . . Heather and Lucy, good grief! But I suppose you could say that now our mutual bemusement is affectionate. They send me 'Heather says' and 'Lucy says' messages via my parents and there is a kindness in this: we love or at least understand each other enough now to leave each other alone.

I usually enjoy looking over the last couple of months and summarising them. It makes me take stock. Some letters home have been like the formation of a resolve I wasn't aware I needed to make until I began to phrase it for someone else. And even this much later, and at this remove, there is the old need to tell my parents about every little achievement. When I was accepted for the diploma course, and then found the job at the surgery to fit around my classes, I wanted them to respond, to write back and say, 'Well done! Who'd have thought? Our Marie—we're so pleased!'

Of course, now that it's become apparent that Joss and I plan to stay together (in what my father insists on calling 'one of those modern De Fective relationships'), Mum has started filling her own letters to me with pointed questions. 'How much longer do you really think you'll be in England, dear? Joss must be so interested in seeing where you grew up, mustn't he? I know I mustn't say it, but if you *were* to start a family, do you think your children would be Londoners?'

I want to tell Mum and Dad about today. They knew Jenny, would know what the sighting meant to me. Suddenly I find I'm missing them both, more than I have before, or more than I've ever acknowledged. Seeing Jen has turned me on the spot.

Now I can't concentrate. I've written down the date at the top of the page, but my forearm rests against the paper and my gaze wanders to the lily in the cylindrical blue glass vase on the mantelpiece. I feel a rush of love for Joss, who gave me the flower two days ago for no particular occasion, and who is probably sinking into sleep in our room, and once more I'm struck by the twin nature of memory. How acute things with Jenny still are. And yet, how foreign that adolescent girl I was has become.

I think again of how as a teenager I swore I would never, ever get married, and of how Jenny and I invented a freedom that meant getting away from all family ties. And of how, when Joss and I met, and in the face of the obliterating tsunami of passion and need, we were each a little afraid for and protective of our independence. So we agreed that marriage was antiquated, antediluvian, antipathetic to our ideas of love. As if nobody had ever been in love before, not the way *we* had. We decided to live together—as if it were any different: as if this way we'd avoid certain facts about two people, persuading ourselves that it was the word *marriage* that caused people to alter and wear and move together, like two pebbles rolling and knocking against one another, and not the whole essence of love. Although we've never married, I couldn't avoid learning about how love works that way, shaping and moulding each person. And how it thickens and deepens; it accretes in layers of finely differentiated colours, so incremental that you'd need to examine it very closely to trace them. Yet the changes are permanent, and so far from what I felt for Blake . . .

What I think of now as the two crucial events—the night at the beach, and meeting Russell and Blake—must have been less than a year apart. They seem now to have come from quite different eras: one before and one after the slow melting of my crippling shyness.

We met Russell and Blake on the night of a senior school dance, arranged between the girls' and boys' colleges, as a beginning of term 'welcome' event. The dance was Jenny's perfect alibi: she wanted to go clubbing instead.

'We're not lying,' she said to me, 'it's still the start of term and we're still dancing—even the entry price is about the same. Come on, Marie. They're just a bunch of kids at the social. It'll be like a whole load of form twos—boys on one side, girls on the other, all dressed like the Brady Bunch. Side parts and frilly skirts. Come *on!*"

I didn't even know what a night club was like, I was that naïve. But I had too many mental images of school dances, and they conformed to Jenny's description. Except that I was one of the girls who had always stuck resolutely to my side of the auditorium or had avoided going at all.

Jenny and I had never been to a dance together, had joined in mutual scorn of the things, although I gathered hers was based on the backwardness of the boys rather than on what I'd once thought of as their intimidating self-assurance. Only during that summer holiday between the sixth and seventh forms had I really found reason to let my nervousness wane—although Jenny's unspoken failure with Dale also had a lot do with it: it had given me confidence in my own ability to judge people. Haughtily I had thought to myself, Who cares if someone is still a *schoolboy* (Jenny's disparaging term)? As long as they're a *good person*.

Jenny and I had found jobs together that summer, at a delicatessen counter in one of Dad's supermarkets. When I had asked him if there would be any holiday vacancies, he'd ruffled my hair. 'Have my uses, do I? Stooping to my level?' But he did find us each a job, and I drove with him to work every day. It became a routine I secretly looked forward to. In the car we would chat—or rather, I'd rabbit on about myself—and he'd either tease me or would chip in with comments that tried to give an overview. 'I know looking ahead to the seventh form seems hard now, Marie, but one day you'll look back and wonder what you were worried about. You kids, you worry about exams and school and friends, but I'm telling you, these years, they're just a blip on your lifeline. A blink. A split second. "All the same in a hundred years", that's what *my* father used to say.' I'd find his opinion either pacifying or infuriating, depending on my mood: yet, in a way that remained unacknowledged then, I always needed to seek it out.

There were several other seasonal employees at our supermarket, all of us bored stiff, caged up for the entire summer, sweating in uniforms, our hands smelling of salami and garlic when other kids were lolling around at the swimming pool or off on long family excursions. Yet every fortnight the pay packet that let us go and buy records or movie tickets brought us release. Jen and I had both started up savings accounts for university, but we'd allow ourselves a portion for luxuries and a social life, much of it spent going out with the kids we worked with. Jenny was patronising about most of the boys ('Still milking pimples,' she said once), but I begged her to come along as my moral support.

'Okay, shy girl,' she laughed.

I certainly felt safer with that group than with the likes of Dale. I was the same age as them, for a start, and nearly as tall. Working together had shown me that they were as ordinary as Gareth and Jonathon. I'd even had to teach one of them how to work the industrial slicing contraption we used for getting thin rounds of meat. He had cut perfectly symmetrical, moon-shaped shreds from his knuckles while cleaning it, and there had been an extraordinary amount of blood. I'd had to grab a tea towel, bind his hand with it, and sit him down as the colour leaked from his face. The way he had stared at his hand as the blood dripped onto the floor had astonished me.

'Oh, but they're such nice boys!' Jenny would quaver at me. And I'd laugh, because she was right, they were nice, and reassuringly safe. But they were also dull. I partly understood their reserve, I suppose, but Jenny grew impatient with their ineptness. Privately, she might have admitted to herself that someone like Dale was too hardened, too cold. But the Delicatessen Dicks, as she openly called them, were definitely too 'wet'. Wasn't there any other option in this place?

Jenny and I each had two weeks off work before starting back at school. Two glorious sunwashed weeks down at the beach, on our own again: making murals in the sand with sea shells, swimming and dragging each other underwater by the ankles, exploring rockpools, sitting on an outcrop, Jen smoking, watching the pollen-gold sunsets, and talking about the year to come. The knowledge that Jenny and I would at least be leaving for university together was both a huge comfort and source of heady anticipation: 'Think what a *brilliant* time we're gonna have!' we'd say, clutching ourselves, clutching at each other, clutching anything else that happened to be at hand close to our chests. As if a Ferris wheel had started—excitement and dread both mounting, mounting—and we sat, trembling, on the brink.

Those two holiday weeks seem in memory much longer than a fortnight. The summer evenings were so warm and tranquil, it was as if time had stretched: we often stayed down at the beach until dusk, waiting for the sky to darken and the moon to appear, like a white bloom opening out under the distant influence of the sun. These were the times when we'd wade into the water again as night came on, and we'd drift on our backs together, imagining we were floating through space, bodiless, quiet.

We went back to school reluctantly, feeling we'd already moved beyond it in many respects. I suppose Jenny's idea about the night club was one way of trying to express that. Her energy finally became infectious. She was driven by an urge to accrue experience, as if it could be saved like bright, minted coins—and I started to feel emboldened by her.

'But what if someone our parents know sees us?' I hedged.

'Our parents' friends at a night club!'

Jenny's incredulity convinced me to go.

After school on the Friday of the dance, we went round to Jenny's house to pick up her clothes before going back to my place. As I waited in the back yard, Jonathon coasted through the gate on his bike, a little breathless from his ride. He hopped off and grinned when he saw me, leaning his bike against a wall.

'Hiya, Flossy,' he said.

'Hiya, Flossy, yourself,' I answered, impressed with my own coolness.

'Off to that dance tonight?'

'Might be.'

'Might be,' he mimicked, and gave two little wriggles of his hips. Hardly knowing I'd decided to do it, I swiped the palm of my hand over the crown of his head; just as suddenly, he grabbed my arm, twisted it behind my back and, as I yelped, quickly pressed himself up closer, to hold me still. 'Did you just do what I think you did?' he asked. 'Did you hit me?'

I started laughing, pretending to struggle to break myself free, although now he held me more gently near to him. I could smell the fresh salty tang of the sweat from his bike ride. His body was incredibly warm, soaking through my clothes like sunshine. I heard the notes of my own laughter melting away as I tried to concentrate on what this emotion was that seemed to be filtering from me, exchanging warmth through all our clothes.

I relaxed my posture slightly. Just then, Marion's face appeared at the kitchen window, almost eye to eye with me. She pushed open the window's iron bracket with one hand.

'What do you think you're doing?'

Jonathon dropped his arms and fell back.

'Are you all right, Marie?' she asked.

'Uh, yeah, I'm fine,' I said. 'It was nothing, really.'

She gave Jonathon a sharp nod as she spoke. 'Quit your arseing around.'

He suddenly seemed to be all big knees and broad shoulders as he slunk me a look before going inside. Marion abruptly shut the window.

Jesus, I whispered to myself. *Jesus God, she's an old cow.*

When Jenny reappeared, I blurted out her name as soon as I saw her. '*Jenny?*'

She was hunting through the contents of her overnight bag. 'Hmmm?'

I looked over at Jonathon's bicycle and the blank kitchen window, and suddenly it all seemed too out of place and embarrassing to explain. 'Oh—nothing. I just thought you were taking ages.' I let the incident drop away, and Jenny shrugged. We hurried off to my house.

We ate an early and polite meal with my parents, acting the charming pair of sweet sixteens they thought we were. We then spent an hour dressing: swapping clothes, doing each other's make-up, teasing each other's hair into high ponytails and setting them with hairspray. We fussed and worried about every little detail—'D'you think I'm too fat?' 'D'you think it's too short?' 'D'you think the lipstick's too bright?'—until we stood side by side and looked in the mirror. Jenny gave an excited wriggle of her hips, just as Jonathon had imitated. 'Let's *do* it!' she said.

But first my father wanted to take a photo. 'Senior dance, eh?' he said. He led us out into the corridor, where we posed, arms around each other, kissing at the camera. He took a picture, then said, 'Now a serious one, just for your Dad, Marie.' We posed again.

I recognised an old tenderness in his face as he looked at me. In a baffling wave of emotion, I thought of our daily car journeys to and from work, and how I would miss them now that I was back at school. Despite my assumption that he'd always loved my sisters more than me, could any reserve between us have been my doing too? I tended to think of him as preoccupied with work, even insensitive at times, with his teasing about my height and weight, or his easy summarising of my stories and problems with 'All the same in a hundred years, *my* father used to say.' But then I was the one who always flew off somewhere, hurrying to be with Jenny, gossiping with her, radiating 'we want privacy' if he or Mum came near. I dropped my arm from around Jen's waist and went to him for a hug. He teetered backwards in surprise, but then kissed me, burying his nose against my ponytail and inhaling. I remembered the way he used to snuffle at me when I was little, pretending to be a horse or a pig who had mistaken me for an apple or truffle, and rubbing his weekend whiskers at my cheek as I squealed, 'Daddy, it's me! It's *Marie!*' And then, as soon as he stopped, 'Daddy, do it again!' He stayed hugging me for several seconds, and bewilderingly I felt like I might cry. I suddenly wanted to stay at home—or else to end the deceit and tell him where we were going.

'Mmm' he said. 'Did you use *all* your mother's hairspray on that head of yours?' Then he pinched me in the ribs. 'Dad's big Amazon, eh?' Spoiling it all.

I pulled away, rejection twisting in me. He wound on the film in his camera, then repacked it into its case as gingerly as if it were a thin champagne flute.

'Don't you go getting Jenny into any trouble now,' he said, putting a hand on Jenny's shoulder and nodding over at me; she laughed up at him in a tone that struck me as strangely grateful. I felt a pang of jealousy, and set to readjusting my ponytail, pushed out of shape where he'd pressed his face against it. That set him off again, goofing around with his own hair in the hallway mirror, saying, in a surreal falsetto, 'Ooh, my pumpkin!' I could have screamed, but Mum appeared in the corridor.

'Let me have a look at you—oh, aren't you a photo opportunity! Don, have you taken a picture?'

'*Yes!*' I snapped. She blinked, but Dad, blockheaded, caught Mum around the waist, asking her why they didn't dance any more. He took the lead and began an elegant foxtrot with her along the hallway—and I just could not work him out. He drove me crazy one minute, then the next I felt this dumb lump in my throat.

Jenny gave them quick applause, and I pulled her by the elbow, wanting to get away. Then we were off, running down the driveway to the bus. We just made it—collapsed into our seats, happy and breathless. When our chests had stopped their deep rising and falling, we gazed out at the darkened streets and the lights that had just come on, barley-sugar orange as they warmed up.

'I always loved this time of night when I was really little,' Jenny said. She pointed up at the lamps. 'I always hoped I'd see the orange lights when we were out driving, picking up my dad from work, before my mum died.' She kept her head turned away from me. 'It's funny, the things that make you think of people.' Jenny had hardly ever talked about her mother. I didn't even know how much she remembered of her. I tried to imagine what it would be like. I wanted to understand, but, searching her profile, I knew any real empathy was as remote as speaking a completely new language. I felt so ignorant, so stupid. She smiled, seemed serene—not troubled, as I'd expected—and, as if reading me, said, 'I think she'd have liked you.' She continued to watch the passing streets. We both fell quiet, and I remember I held myself as still as I could, listening in to Jenny's silence and letting the whole night spread over me, wanting to keep each second close against my skin.

The night club was on the opposite side of town, and we had to change routes half way—the two bus rides making my head swim with nerves and excitement each time we swung around a wide corner—but still we'd arrived too early. Jenny and I were the first people there. As we edged up to the doorway, the bouncer stepped farther out onto the pavement, his burly arms crossed as if over a full bust, his chest and belly evidently expanded by a combination of weights and great steak dinners. He gave a low whistle at Jenny's skirt, which was black denim, and as short as our school gym slips. As he slowly spread his lips into a smile, I was certain we'd been sprung: we were too young to get in; we may as well catch a bus back to the boys' school auditorium and at least be somewhere warm. But the bouncer just widened his smile, and swung open the door. He hadn't said a thing—but his mouth was knowing, amused, and slightly salacious. I gave a quick look behind as we walked up the stairs. He seemed to sit back into his shoulders as if they were a fat easy chair, and he took a long, slow look at our legs as we went up. He reminded me of a German Shepherd watching its dog-roll being unwrapped. Jenny's manner suggested she knew this too, but felt the confident control of the dog's owner.

Something about her made me feel as if she had done all this before—the relaxed way one hand lifted hair loose from where it had slipped under her collar and let it cover her back like a warm, smooth stole. As if she knew the bouncer would be watching, although she hadn't, like me, turned around. All the time I was with her she was taking different lessons from things; sensing some other code, changing at a faster rate, while I watched on, longing.

When we reached the doorway at the top of the stairs, and a booth where we paid the cover charge, I could see that there was no one else inside the bar area. The staff were polishing glasses, and one of the barmen looked up in surprise at our arrival. He checked his watch and spoke to his companion. The other man turned, held up a glass to the light above the bar and pretended to inspect the results of his polishing, but I caught the tilt of his head and the slight nod to the other barman.

'They're watching us,' I whispered to Jenny.

She smiled at me as if there were nothing to worry about. 'We're customers, Marie. They're paid to stand at a bar and watch us.'

She put a hand on my shoulder as if I'd said something dry and witty in reply. She was acting for the men through the doorway. I swallowed the one struggling butterfly that wanted to buffet from my throat to an airy freedom, and followed Jenny in.

She walked right up to the barman who had looked at us over his polished glass. I wished, for just once, that Jenny would show some nervousness. She slipped out the last note left in her purse and leaned one elbow on the bar.

'What are you having?' she asked me.

I said one of the only elegant drinks I knew: 'White wine.'

The barman threw the polishing cloth over his shoulder and raised an eyebrow. 'Medium or dry?'

I was stumped for a moment. 'What?' I looked at Jenny. I thought there was only red or white.

'Dry,' she said to him, and to me: 'I read in *Cleo* that it has less calories.' She browsed over the bottles. 'And a gin and tonic.' That was my mother's favourite six o'clock drink. I should have asked for that.

'Ice and lemon?' he asked.

'Just lemon, thanks.'

He turned away, and I could see Jenny check her reflection in the mirror behind the bottle shelves. She brushed her fingers quickly over her fringe, and caught me looking. 'Just *enjoy* yourself, Marie!'

The barman turned back, passing us the drinks, and as innocuously as if he were filing his nails asked, 'You girls have any age ID?'

I felt my heart start to flee, as if it was trying to get out of the bar ahead of me, but Jenny was already giving him a mock, sulky pout.

'Hell, no. I've gone and left my marriage *and* my birth certificates at home.' She lifted and dropped her shoulders with a big sigh. 'That anti-wrinkle moisturiser I'm using is giving me real hassles. Everyone keeps asking me my age.' She skated the money over the counter surface with the tip of her index finger, and slid both of the glasses towards her, without the least element of challenge, for all the world as if she genuinely believed he'd been flattering her.

He looked thrown, but it was the kind of thrown you see on the face of a man who has just been given an unexpected bonus. There was a moment's uncertainty, then he looked sheepishly at his partner, who went to the till, counted out Jenny's change, then clasped it in his fist in the air. She had to hold out her palm before he would release it.

'Go buy yourself some lollies,' he said.

We took our drinks to the farthest, darkest corner of the room, on the opposite side of the dance floor. As we sat down, my knees trembled.

'Piece of cake,' Jenny said, and raised her glass to me before taking a large swallow.

I'm not sure how long we waited before other people started to arrive, but it seemed interminable. I could feel the barmen watching and discussing us, occasionally punching each other heartily on the arm after apparently particularly pungent remarks. But Jenny was determined to stay aloof. 'Men are useless at guessing a woman's age,' she said. 'Just relax.'

As the first mob of people arrived—about six at once, then a pause, and then group after group who swept the room to find friends, or avoid enemies—I finished my wine, and relaxed into the slightly sleepy haze that I knew from our summer nights of sharing a bottle with Jenny's brothers. At the thought of Jonathon, and our playfight that afternoon, I felt a delicious effervescence at what Jenny and I were doing. *Imagine* if anyone we *knew* found out! I crossed my legs and danced one foot to the track that had come on over the sound system, momentarily full of myself. The barmen were too busy now to bother with us, and I sat captivated by the play of ultraviolet light over Jenny's teeth and freckles: everything she said seemed supremely funny with her face high-lit and luminescent. We looked at each other, laughing, and then Jenny held out her glass.

'We made it,' she said. 'Here's to us.'

'To us, and to always making it,' I answered, and clinked my glass against hers.

Then two men wearing identical clothes—blue Levis, black biker jackets with red plaid linings, black blunt-nosed DM boots—appeared at our table. Each carried a small bottle of lager.

'Do you mind if we sit here?'

That's how things change. People walk in and out of your life, that easily. A stage direction; a sudden shift. The way Joss appeared at the school where I did temp work in London. He walked in as if it were written somewhere in italics: leaning forward, pushing and rushing into the future. Take notice, some entrances say; you may need to remember this later.

We both nodded for them to sit, after exchanging a look. They seemed unconcerned about us in particular: there were simply no more tables left. They sat and talked between themselves, watching the dance floor, heads following newcomers as if they might be expecting someone. I had just begun to pretend a similar disinterest when Jenny leaned over, her breasts pressing against her arms on the table top. One of the guys had brought out a packet of cigarettes—the one whose hair was shaven close and dyed a bright yellow, as if his scalp were warmed by the soft, velvety fuzz of duckling down.

'Would you mind if I had one of your smokes?' Jenny said.

The men both turned towards us with slight surprise, as if they'd forgotten we were there. Then the one with the cigarettes leaned forward, handing her the pack for her to select her own. He offered them to me, and I shook my head. 'Sure?' he asked. He had long black eyelashes: a contrast to his almost glow-in-the-dark hair that made me want to look at him for longer than I would let myself. I could feel myself colour like a leaf turned by the sun. I smiled nervously at Jenny, picked up my empty wine glass and lifted it to my lips before remembering it was finished. His friend, whose shaggy brown mop fell into his eyes, indicated my glass with a nod.

'Can I get you another drink?'

I looked at Jenny, widening my eyes to ask her opinion. She widened hers back at me in a way that I somehow knew was telling me not to ask, not to be so obvious in my hesitation, telling me to detach myself from her, and play a part, now that we were in the company of men. She narrowed her eyes again as she drew in deeply on her cigarette.

'I'm going to the bar anyway.' The man shifted forward a little, fingering in the back pocket of his jeans. Something about his movement hit me. The independence of it. Unencumbered by a small black shoulder bag like Jenny and I were, he was able to move around anywhere, self-contained. Both men sat in their chairs so easily, legs relaxed on the fulcrum of their hips, fitting themselves to as much room as they wanted. And, I noticed, their stomachs were as flat as the backs of their chairs. I'd never noticed before how flat men's stomachs were. Bubbling with the alcohol, I had to stop myself from asking Jenny how they managed to fit all their vital organs inside.

'Well?' The dark-haired man (whose cheekbones, in turn, made me want to stare) was insistent. 'White wine? Dry?'

I nodded, smiled—and felt a new kind of silence rushing in to build up behind it: a warm, urgent ache. I wasn't sure how to say 'yes' any more. The right way to say yes; the best way to say yes; an interesting way to say yes; a way to say yes that would reveal just enough, yet conceal just the same. Perhaps I was as anxious to prove to Jenny, as to him, that I understood the way to do these things.

His friend turned to Jenny. 'What are you having?'

She slowly rid herself of a breathful of smoke. 'G and T, thanks.'

The two men went to the bar together, shifting sideways through the thickened crowd, checking people's faces, touching strangers now and then on the shoulders to get them to move aside. I leaned in to Jenny.

'Jenny, they're *gorgeous!*'

She sat back. 'Marie!'

'Don't you think so?'

She trained her gaze through the crowd and up to the bar. Then she crouched down over the table. '*Yes!*' And she squeezed the knuckles of one of my hands. We talked excitedly. Then she gasped. 'Ohmygod they've started to come back already. Act nonchalant.'

They weaved through the crowd, each carrying two drinks, and set ours down in front of us. I reached for the sequinned bag I had borrowed from my mother, and took out some money.

'No, no, don't bother,' said the blond. 'Get the next round, if you like.'

I faltered, wondering exactly how much we were going to drink, but Jenny made it clear that she was game. 'Thanks,' she said, as she crossed her legs and tapped a small grey log of ash from her cigarette.

The blond man began to rock gently in his seat to the song that had started up. I felt a rush of courage, and raised my voice over the music.

'It's only polite to ask your names, really, seeing you've bought us drinks.'

They looked at each other, and laughed. 'Don't ask if you're only being polite,' said the one who'd handed me my glass. 'We wouldn't want to bore you.'

Jenny rescued me. 'I'm Jenny,' she said, 'And this is Marie.'

Smoothly, and quietly teasing, they presented themselves, and shook our hands.

'Russell,' said the blond, and it seemed to me that he held Jenny's hand for longer than mine. One of the small, strange new suns that had only just risen in my chest had quickly to set again.

'And I'm Blake,' said his friend. He moved the hair from his eyes. He looked questioningly at each of us. 'So, is this a special occasion, or is this what you always do on a Friday night?' The joking edge to his voice said he wondered about our ages.

Jenny shook her head. 'No on both accounts,' she said. 'How about you?'

The men shifted in their seats. 'We come here on a Thursday, usually,' said Russell, 'when it's the Faultline. A friend of mine does the DJing then—the music's better. But even tonight it's really the only decent club around.'

'So you know a bit about music?' I asked.

Jenny gave me a swift look, and I knew that I'd asked something totally naïve. But Russell's quiet smile as he looked down at the hand that twisted his beer bottle was almost bashful.

'Well, yeah, I guess so,' he said. He suddenly seemed younger. 'I do a bit of—you know—guitar. And some song writing. You know, now and then.'

Blake nodded. 'Heard of Lazarus?'

'What, like in the Bible?'

Jenny bit her lip at me, and shook her head—but again Russell and Blake didn't seem to mind.

'Yeah, that's where the name comes from. We're not revivalists as such, but you could say we want a more pure sound, you know, less feedback, more melodic, write lyrics that say a bit more about—well, you know—the soul, for want of a better term, but more than just, like, "Baby I love you" and so on.'

I couldn't tell if he was serious or not, but Jenny stubbed out her cigarette and, as if she hadn't issued either of her body-semaphore warnings to me, asked, 'So you write music together?'

I tried to kick her under the table to say 'traitor'. I got Russell instead.

'Sorry.'

Russell nodded. 'Lazarus is us and two other guys—the drummer and the bassist. Blake does keyboards and we both compose. We've done a couple of gigs at The Pandemonium, actually.'

I could just about hear Jenny's thoughts. These men were musicians. Artistic. Practically rock stars! Was something *happening* to us? *Cleo* said that musicians were always more sensitive and cultivated than other men. I had to hold myself back from doing one of the falling swoons Jenny and I imitated whenever we filled out the magazine's regular questionnaires on 'Your Ideal Man—Would You Recognise Him?'

'Marie plays the piano,' Jenny said. We looked at each other. I couldn't believe she'd said it. I'd given up years ago.

'Yeah?' said Blake. 'Great. You should come and jam with us some time.'

'As in traffic?' I asked. Jenny looked like she'd choke on her drink before she turned it into a proper cough.

'Can I come and listen?' she asked. What was this 'I'? What had happened to us? Jenny was smiling and laughing oddly, and I saw how closely Russell was watching her.

'Yeah—can you sing? You could come and do backing vocals, if you'd audition.' Russell leaned back in his chair.

She gave a playfully scoffing thrust of her chin. 'Do I get a tambourine?'

'If you like.'

Blake swallowed another mouthful of beer, watching me over the top of his bottle. I started to feel a little giddy: the first moment as a swing starts to catapult from the top of its arc. The songs began to blend into one another, as if the whole room were moving through a change in landscape. Russell scraped back his chair. 'Dance?' he said to Jenny. She smiled, lifted her shoulders a little, nonchalant. 'Sure.' And to me, as an afterthought, although he tried to make his voice sound even, he added, 'How about you?'

I already knew, after those short, bantering minutes, that I should leave him to Jenny, or Jenny to him. The memory of Jenny leaving me, as she stepped into Dale's car, flickered through me. I shook my head at Russell—but then, for a disconcerting second, I wondered if I saw a kind of stage fright pass over Jenny's face when I said no. There was something different about her tonight.

Blake stood, and bent over to touch my shoulder. 'Come on,' he said. 'If you're ever gonna be a rock musician you have to show your moves.'

Then Jenny relaxed, stood and went to the dance floor with Russell. I felt a queasy, twisting reluctance. I wanted to tell Blake that he didn't have to ask, just because there were four of us. But I didn't know how to do so gracefully, without the risk that he would feel as if he should then *insist* I get up, while his reservations increased. I sat, hovering at the edge of my seat, trying to summon up the right words, as if paralysed in the middle of a memorised speech—when Blake stood, and held out his hand. I was mortified. I looked to Jenny for a sign of solidarity, but she simply raised her eyebrows at me from the dance floor as Russell whispered something in her ear. She looked at us again, and looked away, but nodded to him, as if she thought that by turning the back of her head to us we couldn't see her response. Their sudden, easy secret-sharing gave me an unfamiliar pang, one that was at once wild and miserly. I ran my palms over my knees.

'Okay,' I said, rising and going to the dance floor, resolutely avoiding Jenny's eye. If she was going to abandon me for some *guy* again—fine. Just fine. I could still have a good time.

I grew breathless and sweaty from dancing in the overheated crush. Now and then I scrutinised Blake, who gyrated and rocked across from me. When he looked up, he gave me a slow grin that sent tingles everywhere over my skin, even under my fingernails, before he closed his eyes and slipped back inside his rhythm.

That night seemed to follow along two simultaneous but opposite timelines. It was over so suddenly, yet so many new sensations were packed into it, that when I lay in bed mulling it over, it was difficult to believe that the night had lasted just a few hours. Blake and I had danced until my calf muscles ached and my throat had gone hoarse from trying to talk over the music. Blake clowned around, spinning on one foot, twisting down to the level of my knees, pretending to play guitar. I wondered if that meant he actually couldn't dance any more than I could. When we talked between songs, I decided that he was the sort of person who listened with his eyes. Underneath that fringe, his enormous brown irises seemed to soak up anything I said like a hungry sponge. He brushed away his fringe once, when we had stopped for a drink at the bar, and then the tenor of his expression changed, so that I glanced over my shoulder to see what was in his sightline. When I turned back—quickly, and so lightly that I couldn't be sure afterwards how it was intended—he brushed back a strand of my hair that had come free from my ponytail, and tucked it behind my ear. He picked up his drink, and moved back over the dance floor. I wanted to grab Jenny and whisper with her in a corner somewhere, but I couldn't find an opportunity. Each time I looked towards her, she was completely focused on Russell.

When a cramp in one of my leg muscles slowed me down and a visit to the bathroom had shown that the kohl-black eyeliner Jenny had helped me to apply had run into two grey lakes under my eyes, I found Jenny sunk into a chair, clasping a glass of water. It felt like I hadn't seen her for hours. I bobbed down so that I could hear her more clearly, and she said briskly that she was too tired to last it out until three, when the club closed. We stood, retrieved our bags, and as if this were a pre-arranged signal, Blake pulled out a pen and Russell a shabby piece of paper from their jeans' pockets. We exchanged numbers, agreeing that the four of us would meet up again. I tried to imitate Jenny's cool detachment.

Jenny and I hailed a taxi, and as I leaned forward to give the driver my address, Jenny poked me in the ribs so hard that I yelped.

'You trying to run us off the road?' The cabby asked. 'Settle down.'

'Sorry.'

He clucked and muttered to himself.

'You!' Jenny continued.

'What?' Now that we were in the deep, creaking car seats, I could hardly keep my eyes open.

'I just about had to drag you in there in the first place, you were so nervous, and then I just about had to drag you out again!' She gave me another nudge.

'What? What do you mean?'

'It's half past one, Marie—the senior dance ended at twelve. If we wake up your parents, or if they're still awake, we'll be in deep shit.'

'Why didn't you tell me?'

'I was trying! But you were so involved with Blake, making eyes at him . . .'

That was ripe. How did she think she'd been acting?

'I was not making eyes at him! You ignored me for most of the night! The reason I danced with Blake in the first place is because you'd completely lost interest in me. You were making eyes at Russell.' I slumped further down in the seat in a huff.

'Marie, you've had too much to drink.'

'Have not.'

'And anyway . . .' Jenny poked me again.

'What?' I turned abruptly to her.

'That's not the *only* reason you stayed dancing with Blake. Is it? And I never said I wasn't making eyes at Russell. I was. And I wasn't *ignoring* you. I was trying to make sure you got to talk to Blake properly. I didn't want to barge in at the wrong moment.'

Or for me to I barge in on you, I thought. Would we always go so weird on each other because of men?

'Oh yeah?' I said.

'Yeah.'

'Huh.'

'Whadda y'mean, "huh"?'

'I was cramping your style.'

Jenny puckered her lips. 'Marie, my style cannot be cramped.'

I hooted, but gave up, and snuggled around in the seat again, slipping against her as the cab rounded a corner. I was asleep instantly—Jenny had to shake me awake, so that we could add together our last shavings of silver and copper to pay the driver. When the cab pulled away, we stood outside my house, fully anticipating that a light would go on and a curtain would be shunted back to show a tired, pillow-creased face frowning out, cross with a mixture of sleep and worry. But the house stayed shadowed, a slumbering mound in the dark. I slid my key into the lock, and the noise seemed to ricochet like a slot machine thundering out coins; we froze on the spot, as if we expected something to rise up and bellow. Then I slid open the door gently, gently, and our feet shushed down the carpet, into my room, where we undressed in silence.

Throughout our tentative preparations for bed, excitement and a pretend fear throbbed at my throat. We let each other in and out of the room on the way to the bathroom as if keeping watch: protecting not just ourselves from being apprehended (late, betraying trust, anything could have happened to us, they were worried sick—all those legitimate claims that loved ones make, instantly illegitimate upon your reappearance), but also protecting our secret—the fizzing jubilation of meeting Blake and Russell—from being sullied too soon by having to describe it. It was as if the events would be altered by having to explain them, as if hope would corrode in the air of speech.

Now, so many of our movements that evening seem like an unthinking rehearsal for the night, many months later, when I had to let Jenny into my room unexpectedly. Padding the carpet, silencing doors, hurried sign language, being constantly alert to the proximity of the sleeping bodies of my parents in a nearby room: we could have been refining subterfuge and silence like an art, though the fear we tiptoed in that night was no more than a game.

The next morning, my mother came and tapped on the door at eleven, bringing us her tray with mugs of tea, apple juice, and even a pink carnation bud leaning its chin out over the rim of a white china vase. Jenny and I had been sound asleep, but mum chirped, sounding as irrepressible and unaware as a teetotaller starting the motor mower at eight o'clock on a Sunday.

'I heard you stirring!' she lied.

'Oh, wow, tea—thanks, Mum.' I struggled up to humour her.

Jenny groaned. 'Oh, Jesus.' She rolled over, opened an eye and heaved herself up onto one elbow. 'Oh, wow, tea,' she echoed.

Mum plopped herself down on my bed, and the reverberations made me shudder a little. My first real hangover, and I had to act as well. 'Us old things went off to sleep early last night,' she said, handing out mugs. 'We didn't even hear you come in. We must have gone out like lights! You *were* good not to wake us.'

Jenny and I murmured, and took simultaneous sips of tea to straighten out any hint of a smirk—which must in itself have looked suspicious. Mum certainly picked up on something. She wriggled herself a more comfortable hollow on top of my covers, and cuddled her own cup of tea closer to her chest. 'Soooo—tell me all about it,' she said. 'Did you meet someone?'

Jenny concentrated on her tea in a way that said this was one occasion on which she was not going to help me out.

'Well—' I wished she'd leave us alone, but there was no chance of that. I looked hard at my mug handle, running my thumb over a small chip in the enamel. 'We both met someone, actually. But they weren't exactly at the dance.' Mum's face stayed expectant. I couldn't look at Jen. 'I mean, they're not at the boys' college, but they were at the dance—at the dance we were at.'

'They're musicians,' Jenny blurted, back in the relay after all.

And as if we'd already prefabricated our story, I had it. 'That's right, they're musicians, and they were helping to run the dance floor—you know—they took turns at DJing and so on.'

'Really?' Mum began to look a little worried. 'How old are they?'

'I don't know,' I said, which was true.

'We forgot to ask.' Jenny's hands around her mug had a praying effect.

'We just got on so well, it didn't seem to matter.'

Mum didn't seem very appeased. The delicate lines across

her forehead had gone into a complex tangle. I could sense an advice session coming.

'Mum, it's okay! Don't look so worried! You look like you're trying to knit a jersey with your face!'

Jenny snorted up some tea and spluttered it all over the bodice of her nightgown.

'Marie!' Mum pushed my hand away. She whisked a handkerchief from her cuff, and handed it to Jenny, whose explosion had threatened to capsize the campbed we always set up for her when she stayed the night. I kept talking.

'They used to go to the school,' I said, and found myself becoming alarmingly elaborate about what they'd done there. As I constructed more and more, it seemed to get easier and easier, and I ended up having to restrain myself as Jenny's eyes widened into round astonishment. But my mother expected a lot from one night. She even asked for Russell's and Blake's last names, as if it were a test of credibility and reputation. I knew why she asked—she wanted to go through the files in her head to see if she could align the men we'd met with Dr So-and-So's nice sons, or some nursing colleague's nephews, or a patient's promising brothers . . . anything that might give her a sense of security. At the time it exasperated me; I understood it as a kind of social climbing. Now I've realised there was less in it of that than anxiety.

It was only years later—years and years—that she told me there had been someone else before my father. Someone she'd been engaged to when she was still very young, and who'd hurt her badly, although she still wouldn't tell me how. 'How many ways are there to hurt a young girl?' she'd said when I tried to delve. 'And what matters in the end? The way it was done, or the outcome?' Her secrecy about this, so uncharacteristic of her, puzzled me, yet I couldn't do much else but respect it. 'I mended,' she said, 'although not for a long time. It was almost five years before I met your father.'

If she had known that Russell and Blake were 'nice boys', perhaps she could have worried less about what permanent distortions they might be branding on the warm red wax of our memories. It didn't occur to me that morning that my mother might know more about our vulnerability than we did. She has never told me what happened to her. I still wonder, but a letter hardly seems the place to ask.

I left her with a patchy picture—two musicians, perhaps first year university age (though I said that only to comfort her, thinking it an association that would make them sound earnest and safe). Ex boys' collegiate, very polite, very talented (their own band! Hadn't she heard of Lazarus? No, we didn't know how they made a living, but then they were university age . . .); very handsome . . . and *yes*, Mum, we had agreed to meet as a group, we'd tell her When and Where we were meeting, no need for the lecture on self-defence.

In the end, she was just pleased that I seemed to have finally left behind my image as a prematurely aged and serious St Jerome. It was a pleasure that excused my meeting a slightly offbeat, perhaps unsuitable man—not a boy—in my first real foray into the world of the opposite sex. She patted my knee, which lifted the bedclothes into a tent, and said, as a sign of acceptance, 'If you girls get up and shower, I'll make you pancakes for breakfast.' As if it were our joint birthday and we were both eight years old. How I loved her, underneath all my adolescent scratchiness.

About two weeks passed before we heard from Blake or Russell. It seemed like years. I found excuses to loiter in the centre of town after school, hoping I might bump into Blake— thinking a rock musician would of course be living in the centre of things. It was, I thought, simply bad luck that I never saw him.

Looking back, that absence seems to indicate one of the odd qualities of our town. For months there, you can see the same person in the same place at the same time, so that he or she acquires the permanence of a building or a flagpole, helping to give the town its particular character. A friendly town, the locals will tell visitors. Yet you can also live there for years, and never run into the people you know most intimately. Months can go by without seeing more casual acquaintances, either, so that when your paths do happen to cross, it feels like a reunion. As if you had lost each other and the greetings are more like reconciliations, although your surprise at encountering each other again counterfeits other emotions, like affection and understanding. After the hellos, where-have-you-beens, I-thought-you-must-have-moved-ons, people walk away with a sense of diminishment, appraising their achievements—'*Should I have moved on?*'—and with a sneaking sense that the spontaneity on both sides was actually less than pleasure. Then, more months go by without further encounters. It's as if people vanish.

I already knew that the streets of our town worked like this: like an Escher illusion, sketched in time dimensions. Still, I deliberately suggested long walks to Jen after school. Hair in a teased ponytail, wearing a short black skirt, black tights and blue denim jacket, as if I thought the ritual of dressing up could help to summons an encounter with Blake. In that heady fortnight of imagining, I'd have tried any love potions. At lunch, like a twelve-year-old, I twisted my apple stalks, saying a letter of the alphabet on each turn, hoping it would come off with the second letter, or that the alphabet would run all the way through and I could have a second chance. A, B, B for Blake, it was meant to be. Usually I wished his name began with something later in the alphabet.

Jenny was the first to get a phone call—from Russell. Through her, arrangements were made for the four of us to get together. I was disappointed that Blake hadn't phoned me, but excited at the prospect of meeting him again. With a date and time fixed—the next Friday night at a coffee bar to start with—the weeks of waiting didn't seem so bad.

When we met, I was so nervous that the five-dollar note I held over to the cashier as I paid for coffees was trembling. I couldn't see my hand shake, but I willed it to stay steady. I felt a tremor at the back of my neck, as I often had when I was singled out in class and told to answer a question: when it felt as if a whole muscular chord in my neck had been struck, like a string deep in the body of a piano. Now it seemed as magnified as a full-blown medical syndrome. But when I whispered to Jenny, 'Oh, *God*, can you see my head shaking?' she looked at me as if I were odd. 'No,' she clipped, and briskly slid her cup towards her.

Russell and Blake were already there, the evening paper spread between them and the table cluttered with small stainless steel teapots, milk jugs and white ceramic cups. As I walked over a pace or two behind Jenny, balancing my cup with as much elegance as someone in an egg and spoon race, I shot them a quick look—and in that instant became queasily certain that there was something uncomfortable in Blake's posture. His head had lowered quickly just as I raised my glance. When we reached the table, both he and Russell were warm, but Blake's greeting was equally so for us both. After that, he mainly shared eye contact with Russell—that is, when he did look up from the entertainment listings in the newspaper. Measuring all this with an accuracy that I wished I was less sure of, I concentrated on sipping my coffee. Jenny was bright and chatty, laughing enough for both of us, and she and Russell seemed as calm as two people visibly intrigued by each other could be.

We ended up seeing a film. I sat between Blake and Jenny, and half way through the movie, with a quiver of electricity, I felt Russell's fingertips accidentally brush my shoulder as he put his arm around Jenny. It was as if the outline of my body had become pronounced with anticipation; someone had drawn a line around me in a halo of fluorescent light. But the feeling cooled. Blake occasionally looked at me, to share his laughter at some line in the movie, but his hands stayed preoccupied with popcorn.

After the picture, we went to a bar where there was meant to be a live reggae band, but the musicians spent ages sound-checking before they shuffled away because some of the equipment was down. There were a few shifty-seeming exchanges between Blake and one of the band members. The acquaintance was slump-shouldered, long-haired, stubbly, with a pouch of slack skin under his chin. They asked each other what they had been up to, topping each other's answers with 'Good, good' in a way that suggested that neither of them had listened to the other's reply. The other man's eyes slid over to me, then back to Blake. He asked a disinterested filler question, 'Out with a couple of friends, eh?' and Blake's glance nervously skipped to somewhere else in the room. 'Yeah, yeah,' he repeated. A chain of uncomfortable, equivocal intonations. I excused myself for a moment, and went to the Ladies'. The bar had a wild west theme: a black silhouette of a woman doing the can-can was stuck askew on the toilet door. Cheap and phoney. Not at all like the world I'd imagined *going out* with someone would conjure up. The whole night was one big fake. I banged through and locked myself in a cubicle, cursing into my palms, wishing Jenny could feel the unexpectedly icy wall that Blake presented instead of being so one hundred percent absorbed in Russell's every story about himself. Angry tears sprang up, but I willed them back in. I breathed as deeply as I could bear in the sickly lemon-scented toilets, then deliberately bit a lip until it bled. The sting was a comforting focus as I walked back out to the table.

Someone had chosen jukebox records when the band had packed up and a few people—the most drunk, but also, to my dismay, Jenny and Russell—were dancing between pushed-aside central tables. Blake toyed with a beer and had brought out the newspaper again as a prop. I slid into the side booth, allowing him a thin-lipped and, I hoped, utterly detached smile. A defence seemed to drop. He folded the paper and leaned onto the table top. I saw his Adam's apple rise and fall like the level in a barometer as he swallowed.

'Russell tells me he's wanted to get in touch with Jen a few times this week,' he said. He gazed at them dancing for a moment. 'He seems pretty keen, don't you think?'

I was thrown, instantly preferring the feigned indifference we seemed to have been collaborating in so far. 'I guess it's too early to tell, really,' I hedged.

He spun a beer cap, then tapped it several times on the table top, as if calling his thoughts to attention. 'I've been thinking, since we met at the club.' He swallowed again. 'Doesn't the age gap worry you at all?' There was something uncomfortable about the way his jaw had set, but he was trying to be—what was it?—gentlemanly. To let me down carefully but firmly, just the way magazine articles always instructed.

I felt as if the room had filled with breathable air again. 'How old are you and Russell?'

'He's nearly nineteen, I'm twenty-one.'

One of my sisters was about to turn twenty-one, but the way he said it made it sound generations older. The tone of his voice had flicked a switch, plunged the scenes of Blake and myself—which, for two weeks, had been sending me off to a sweet sleep at night—into an empty-cinema darkness. I tried to win him back.

'If it doesn't worry either of them,' I said, 'it doesn't worry me.' Blake shifted in his seat and, strangely, sympathy welled in my throat. 'But I know what you mean. I guess seventeen must seem so young to you . . .' He looked crushed, the dark red in his cheeks like petals ground under someone's boot heel. It seemed I had just put him on the spot when I had intended to let him off the hook while sounding more mature than the young kid he thought I was. To my consternation—I couldn't predict anything about this situation—Blake's hand moved over the newspaper, and with one finger he traced over the small hills and valleys of my knuckles.

'You're very beautiful,' he said.

I froze. What on earth was he doing? Why was he saying that?

'Really. Really. I wanted to say—I know you must have had certain ideas about us all meeting tonight, after the club and so on. But—you know—' He followed some invisible, fleeting thing in the air, then he scrutinised me. 'You've got your whole life ahead of you, you're young. And at the moment, I'd just be bad for you. It wouldn't work.'

So what could he see in me that it would be so 'bad' to change? He thought I was square. Naïve. Too straight. Too good. Too everything. Not like Jenny. Russell must have known Blake wasn't interested. Why did he ask him along? Why did Jenny ask me? She was just using me as an excuse to come out—'I'm going out with Marie, Dad.' I wanted to cry. God, my expectations must have been screaming out from the way I'd moved and talked. I wished he'd carried on being quietly dismissive instead of so frank. I was humiliated. He made it sound as if he knew I would be heartbroken, when I'd been trying so hard not to show what a cocktail of ebullience and shyness I was acting under. I was easy to see through, had tried to rush in to something, and he knew. I found a nasty little resentment flourishing in me. Blake squeezed my hand again.

'Hey, you okay?'

'What makes you think I was so keen to go out with you in the first place?' I asked. I couldn't look him in the eye.

He breathed out in a short, constricted push, a half-hearted laugh, and he fell to toying with the sugar bowl on the table. He measured out perfectly shaped white slopes, then let them trickle off the spoon slowly, sifting for a tiny piece of gold, a missing sentence the shape of a sugar grain.

'The thing is,' he said, 'I'm not round here for much longer. I'm moving up north in a few weeks, to look for work, and I've had an offer from a friend who needs a keyboardist in a more established band.' He let the spoon fall back into the bowl. 'I just thought I should let you know, in case you'd got the wrong idea.'

Getting and giving the wrong idea. As I lifted my eyes to look at him, we both knew which moment in the night club he meant. How many ideas there must be contained in the smallest of gestures, the touch of a hand to a cheek. All those mixed-up, right and wrong ideas, jostling like atomic particles in the blush that the heat of a hand can leave behind.

Jenny and Russell had given up on finding enough space to dance properly; they weaved over through the other dancers, and asked us if we wanted anything to drink. Jenny was flushed and a little sweaty; Russell had rolled up his shirt sleeves. He ran his hand through his blond hair, which darkened as he spread the dampness back from his brow. As his arm swept backwards, I saw how the muscles in his arm flexed.

This new, insistent awareness of male beauty just made things worse. I said no, I didn't want anything to drink, and that if everyone didn't mind, I'd leave them to it and get back home. Blake's eyes widened, and Jenny looked as if I'd slapped her. She held my arm.

'No, Marie, you should stay. What's the matter—aren't you having a good time?'

That she could so easily overlook my discomfort just because Russell was there sent a wish to wound her hurtling through me. I resisted it as hard as I could, but still let free a curt 'No, I'm not!' Her lips parted slightly in surprise.

'It's okay. You can carry on without me. I'll give you a call,' I said to Jenny. I turned to Russell, and then to Blake, and said as sarcastically as I dared, 'Lovely to see you again,' and shrugged on my jacket. As I walked away, I was aware of all three of them arrested in the same positions, watching me go.

'Stuff them,' I thought to myself. 'What's so bloody wrong with going home when you're bloody fed up?' I swung out of the pub and into the Friday night crowd. Someone elbowed me, 'Frigging fed up, fed up, fed up.' And I thought, God, I *hate* this place. I hate it here. Somehow I got myself home, though my eyes stung as if Blake and I were still trapped in our awkward confessions, with Jenny removed from me, off in a corner with someone else.

Jenny phoned the next day, and I was terse about Blake, saying he'd jumped to conclusions; it was really strange, I hadn't even made my mind up about him, and he'd made me feel really uncomfortable. Besides, if he wasn't interested, why did he come along? She was quiet. I wondered why she phoned, if she wasn't going to try to sympathise. We hung up, agreeing limply to see each other soon. Stuff it anyway, I thought. I want some time on my own.

Oh, I was stung. I tested my heart like a medic: 'This is a broken heart,' I thought, and pressed my hand over my breast, as if, like a tongue that probes into the mushy-plum gap left behind by a lost tooth, I could judge the pain better that way. But of course I healed quickly: ridiculously so. I treated myself all weekend to old comforts, like good books, a family-sized chocolate bar to suck on, bubble baths, lazy TV—even scooting over on the couch to rest my head against Dad's upper arm, as he sat with his hand on Mum's knee while she knitted. Dad murmured, 'Still not too big for hugs, eh?' and I let them both cosset me. But by Sunday afternoon, I missed Jenny. She was all my private life. Was I going to let some guy she'd known for all of about sixty seconds ruin that? We'd been through worse together. It wasn't like she'd left me stranded on a beach for some grease-monkey.

When I called, Jen was out. I was appalled. I always knew what Jenny was doing, where she was going—I was usually there with her. Dad found me by the phone, trying to form a word of protest. 'Catching flies?' he said.

Dad said he was heading out to the back garden to dig over the compost in the late-afternoon sun. He was wearing old baggy black tracksuit bottoms, a maroon v-neck sweater and an embarrassing turquoise-coloured towelling sunhat. He started fossicking around in a cupboard for gumboots. 'Going to come and help me, cherub?' That particular tone he used: telling me, disguised as asking.

We'd had countless weekends of simmering looks when I was a teenager. 'Time we toughened you up,' he'd say. 'Come and help me in the garden. Burn off calories. Build those muscles.' I would excuse myself, saying I had homework to do or had made plans to see Jenny, then leave him to whip out the lawnmower's stubborn starter cord again and again, as if he'd quite like to yank me back in the same way, though the resolutely bland look on his face was meant to make me grateful that he was too decent a bloke to do so. But perhaps he felt hurt, and not annoyed. On such occasions he'd spend a particularly long time doing the strip of grass outside my bedroom window, back and forth, back and forth, until the raw patches of dirt showed through the poor green stubble, like eczema. I was always determined not to look at him through the window as he went to and fro, to and fro, rubbing his salty virtue into my selfishness.

But that night I had nothing better to do. I sighed, heaving myself out of the chair by the phone, and searched for my own gumboots in the cupboard. They stank, and the white insides felt refrigerated on my bare feet. I struggled to get them on, and trailed after Dad, whose quickened, bouncy walk looked like a party charade of 'jaunty'. He whistled, his big boots flapping around his calves with hollow slaps. He ducked into the shed, and brought out a pitchfork and spade. 'Which one?' His face was bright with expectation, as if he were offering me a choice between mint chip or hokey pokey ice-cream. I groaned.

'God, Dad, it's just the compost heap—it's not bloody Disneyland.'

He struck the concrete path with a chilly scrape of prongs and blade, leaning on them like malevolent-looking walking sticks. 'What the hell's the matter with you, Marie? You're seventeen, for Christ's sake. Quit the insolent kid act.'

I looked aside to the vegetable patch, avoiding his eyes. I was pissed off, but there was something ridiculous in arguing with a man in a turquoise towelling hat. His hair peeked out here and there, like the feelers of some brown sea creature exploring beyond its shell. There was another clunk from his tools.

'You're up and down like a yo-yo. What's got into you this weekend?'

I thrust my hands into my pockets and screwed up my mouth. He thought I was going to talk about emotions when he snapped at me like that? I felt my toes cross inside my boots and my fists scrunch up in my pockets, holding back my reactions. Despite myself, I could also feel my chin trembling. Just proving him right: I was swinging all over the place.

He changed tactics. I felt an arm go around my shoulders, and he tugged me closer to him.

'Hey?' he said. 'What's up, Mary-lee?'

It worked. I couldn't help leaning into him, looking down at my boots. A little red money spider, small as an asterisk and only just visible from that height, scampered over the toe of one foot. They were meant to bring you luck and money if they ran over your skin, he and Mum had said when I was little. He gave me another squeeze, and handed me the pitchfork.

'Is it this young man your mother tells me you've met?' he asked. His voice had gone a little gruff, as if he found it difficult to ask. Its awkwardness released the pressure from me like an unstoppered fizz bottle.

I knocked at some weeds that had flung their spiked skirts out over a wide crack in the concrete. 'Not really. It's more Jenny. Nothing really happened with Blake. It was kind of over before it even started, if you know what I mean.'

He nodded sagely, and bent to scoop up the weeds I'd loosened. He crumbled the small beads of dirt from the roots, hitting them against his thigh.

'Felt you didn't have much in common?' he asked.

'Well—he felt that.'

Dad frowned, and put his muddy fingers on my shoulder. 'Obviously a jerk,' he said. A patch of warmth stole into my throat and spread.

'Yeah,' I said. 'Obviously a jerk.'

Dad grinned, and patted me on the back. We headed off to the compost bin, which was really just a narrow gap between our shed and the neighbours' stone wall that had been bricked off at knee height, in three sections. The idea was that you moved compost into a new section as it decayed, until the last third was filled with rich, pungent muck while the first was filled with fresh clippings and peelings. Sometimes the smell was sweet, like hay and flowers. Other times, there was a terrible stench, like rank weed, rancid butter and rotten eggs all mixed in. I bagsed the first, fresh section. We climbed on top of the separate heaps, and I began to shovel drying matter forward while Dad turned it over in the second bin to get air circulating. Spiders, beetles and slaters ran free up the face of the neighbours' wall— a tiny exodus of startled creatures, taking nothing with them, as Dad had always instructed for fire drills and natural disasters. The late afternoon sun was still warm, turning the shed windows silver as we worked.

'So,' Dad dug and lifted, talking to me while he concentrated on his task. 'What is it with Jenny?'

I felt calmer now, the physical exercise working out my mood. 'Did you know she met someone at the same time?'

'Yup.'

'She seems to be pretty interested in him, and he's keen as well.' I stopped digging for a second, to breathe in the smell of daphne that had just washed through me, as if the sun had moved directly to the bush in our neighbours' yard and was brewing the flowers. Dad noticed that I'd stopped, and squinted into the lemon-coloured light, his chest rising and falling more than usual from the effort of turning the compacted section. He propped himself against the shed's rear wall and took off his hat, using it to wave small, lazy fruit flies away from his face. His eyes stayed squinted as he looked at me.

'You're keen on the same chap?'

I gave a small 'huh' of laughter, and thought of Russell. He was gorgeous, but Jenny was more his type. Anyone could spot it. Jenny had something extra—or perhaps I should put it differently. Everything about Jenny was streamlined; I was the one who had the extra, the excess—the awkwardness, shyness, puppy fat, the too-straight hair, everything I wanted to discard, like unneeded outer leaves.

'No,' I said slowly. 'It's not that. It's more—Jenny's my only real friend. She's the only one who's ever really cared about me.'

Dad butted in. 'We care about you, your mother and I—and your sisters.' I twisted the handle of my pitchfork. My sisters? Oh yeah, *right*, Dad. He waited, then said, 'Is it not the same?'

I shook my head, and took a quick look at him. He was wounded.

'It can't be the same, can it?' I said. 'I mean, you guys didn't choose me—you know, didn't meet me and decide you liked me, just because of the way I was, did you? You just *had* me.'

I was trying to explain, but he had that bee-stung puppy look of his. 'We didn't have to like you, though,' he said. 'Some parents don't actually like their kids.'

Of course I knew that. He had it all tangled up. Hadn't I consistently witnessed Marion, Gerald and Jenny? I tried again.

'I love you guys and everything, you know that. That's not what I meant.'

He looked self-conscious. Like the boy he was in his old school photos: head always tipped to the side, one shoulder a little lifted, as if he were always expecting someone to cuff him on the ear.

'What do you mean then?' he asked. He started digging again.

'Just that Jenny's my only friend—and if she starts to see Russell, I won't be *her* only friend any more, will I?'

'Well,' Dad said, in the languid, preparing way he had. 'You might find she has less time for you now and then. But the thing is, at your age, boys do tend to come and go. She won't think like that now—why should she? It would spoil the fun. But that's a fact. And a friend she's had for—what, nearly three years? It just wouldn't be like her not to need to talk to you still.'

I was amazed. Despite our early morning car rides to work over the summer, I'd never thought of talking to him about such things before: Mum had always said we could tell her anything, and I'd gone to her first, somehow surmising it meant that Dad was less approachable. But perhaps I'd helped to close him off, close him up, by assuming: *he just wouldn't understand*. I remembered that hug we'd had on the night of the so-called senior dance photo. And then how he'd screwed it up: just made me want to escape with Jen, away from his predictable jibes. Maybe he'd felt he'd missed something too.

'Do you know what I'd bet?' he said, and lobbed a spadeful of stringy, brown compost from the bottom of the pit into the last section. 'I'd bet she'll sometimes need to talk to you more. Having a boyfriend's quite a thing.'

'You think so?'

His spade made a chipping sound as it scraped against the brickwork. 'I might be a man,' he said, 'but I'm not a jerk.' And then it came flying at me. A big wadge of soil and roots, a spadeful of dirt that hit me, bullseye, in the gut, and scattered, filling the loose tops of my gumboots and spilling down inside to litter my feet.

'Gotcha!' He made a village-idiot's face at me, and we started shovelling compost all over each other—until he suddenly scooped up a spadeful of earthworms which squirmed away as if they were in pain. He held them under my nose, crooning, '*Mary-lee, Mary-lee, got to eat earth worms for tea!*' I hollered, jumped out of the heap and ran around the yard to find the garden hose. I came around the opposite side of the shed and blasted him, right smack on the back with a hard jet, my thumb held over the nozzle to give it perfect aim.

'You little wretch!'

I dropped the hose—it snaked wildly, spraying me as well, and I ran bellowing at the top of my voice, all around the garden, trying to get my gumboots off to hurl at him before I got inside. Mum threw open the back door.

'What the blazes is going on out here?'

I ran yelling towards her, and clung on to her in the doorway. 'Pax! Pax! Safe zone! Safe zone!'

Dad swung the hose around, and it sent a braided silver arc spanning over the entire yard. In the last of the sunlight, a coloured mist rose from it. Mum and I stood there, hypnotised, seeing Dad behind the arc and the mist, his body strong and outlined. Then the water hit, knocking and clattering against the back door's window, pizzling all over the porch and drenching us both completely.

The next day at school I kept watching Jenny hard, trying to decide whether she behaved differently. I asked myself if she looked older, more sophisticated, or bored: with me. After all, meeting a guy was one of the things she—we—had been waiting for. Already I missed the strange, giddy feeling that encountering Blake had given me: that blissful disorientation, as if I were inside a life that wasn't quite my own. I thought Jen would show something of what I'd felt: but she was mostly the same, except that in the silences that came now and then as we ate our lunch her attention wafted away, as if part of her filled with air and floated off, coming back to me only when I said things twice.

As I'd guessed, she had seen Russell the night before. And she'd told Marion and Gerald she was meeting me.

'You don't mind, do you, Marie? They trust you, that's all. I'd do the same for you.' I suppose I was glad she did still need me.

She and Russell had met for a coffee: 'And I couldn't sleep after that! Too much caffeine, I guess. I lay there, going over and over all the things he'd said, my head buzzing with colours, kind of like, each time I closed my eyes, I had my face pressed up to a TV screen, and there were thousands of dots and sparks.

I'm so tired!' But I could tell that her exhaustion was in a new emotional pitch.

Russell wasn't just in a band, she told me; he also worked in a music store, eight till four, five days a week. At nineteen, he was already a 'junior assistant floor manager'. I wondered what that was exactly.

'Are you seeing him again tonight?'

'No, he's got a jam session on.'

'I still don't get why they call it that,' I said. 'I mean, what a weird word.'

Jenny flicked an apple core off her desk and on to someone else's. 'Maybe it's because all the instruments mix together in whatever order, until you sort out what they're doing.'

'Maybe. Just makes me think of something sweet and sticky.'

'Like kisses.'

'Oh, *what*? Is that what it was like with him?'

All her freckles darkened, then almost disappeared as she blushed, and she gave a laughing, sideways movement with her whole body. I'd never seen her like this before. We were sitting on tables in the common room, and she clasped her hands between her knees, squeezing them together, kicking her legs a little. She tipped her head back, and looked up at the ceiling. 'Yes!' she sang, up to the electric lights. Then she hunched her shoulders down, and leaned in to me. 'He'd had some carrot cake at the café. It had thick cream-cheese icing.' She measured a gap in the air between her thumb and finger, the size of a textbook. 'I could taste little crystals of it when he kissed me.' She bit her lip, as if holding herself back from whirling off in ecstasy.

'*Really?*' I said. 'Oh my God, Jenny, I'm seventeen, and I have *never* been kissed! I'm a *reject!*'

She laughed her scaling laugh. 'Kind of like the song! But you're not over the hill. Yet.'

I reached over and grabbed a fat handful of her hair. It felt soft, yet sprung. 'I'll drag on it,' I threatened.

She leaned in, trying to keep the lank of hair slack so it wouldn't tug. 'Okay, okay, okay, I promise to tell you something, I promise to tell you something!'

I held on. 'What?'

'Let go first.'

I let go of her hair, and Jenny's hands encircled mine.

'Kissing Russell is the first time I've actually *liked* it.'

My mouth dropped open. 'Really?'

'Honest to God-ness.'

I reached out and gave her hair a swift pull anyway. We started squealing, giggling and tussling like kids, but I managed to seize hold of her wrists and make her look me straight in the eye.

'Do you think you'll go on the pill?'

Those words—*the pill*—sounded so risqué to me. I remembered the metallic sheet of little minty tablets I had found in my mother's dresser when I was small. I thought I'd found something to eat, hidden away like the trays of Cadbury's chocolates from my aunts at Christmas. 'What are *these*, Mummy?'

My mother had snapped up the foil sheet from my hand. 'They're nasty,' she'd said. 'They're medicine—they're not to eat. If little girls eat them, they can get very, very sick. Do you understand?' I did. I had already been told the fable of nasty things many times by my father. The fable of a boy called Jeremy and his little sister Jemima, who one day found bottles in a cupboard full of things like soap, gasoline and bad medicine. They had drunk it all, Dad said, and had to have their stomachs pumped, which would hurt like a horse-kick in the belly or the worst possible tummy bug. *And*, he'd said, in a voice like darkened houses where things followed you, Jemima had *died*. *Died* was evidently something that made parents extremely angry. I had slipped from the stool at my mother's dressing table, and padded out of her room, feeling guilty that I'd asked.

The pill—now it had an air of intrigue.

'I don't know,' Jenny said. 'I think condoms would be easier. You can get them anywhere—you don't even have to go to the doctor. If I went to lechy Dr Clements, he'd tell Dad, and I'd be for it. And besides, you wouldn't have to remember condoms every day, only when you needed them.'

That sounded sensible. I was always forgetting things you'd think I'd be used to remembering every day: gym gear, economics books, chemistry notes, bus pass. I carefully stored up the information.

'So where would you buy them? Not Middleton's. He'd probably tell your dad too.'

'Course not. The urgent pharmacy in town. They have lots of different staff shifts there. Or you can get them at vending machines some places. I've seen them. You could even get them at the family planning clinic, only your mum's friend works there sometimes. I've seen her go in. So I'd probably not go there, really.'

I was impressed. She'd already thought everything through—every tiny detail. Carefully. She knew exactly what she was doing and she was pragmatic and informed in advance. That foresight circles and circles in my head now. For other reasons.

Each lunch time, and after school on the days when she wasn't seeing Russell, Jen told me how things were going. I felt as if she were the only one who had stories to tell. I didn't go out with her to meet Russell and his friends, as I could have done. I was nervous about seeing Blake again before he moved north, and didn't want to intrude on Jenny's and Russell's time. Avoidance became a pattern, and I turned back into an earlier version of myself: more studious, and a little more solitary, as I had been at thirteen or fourteen.

But Dad was right: although Jen was taking off on her own, she still needed someone else there.

I remember the longing I felt when Jenny told me some things about her relationship with Russell. Was it the same as jealousy?

I suppose there was something of that in it. But if it was, it was envy of Russell. So often I wanted to have Jenny to myself, and I felt let down when he appeared. Yet something else inside me wanted to push forward into the future, to find out how I would feel in Jenny's position. It was a pressure at my throat and high in my chest, as if something hot and rich were being held out to me, just far enough away that I could sense the tantalising fragrance and heat.

That longing was there when Jenny told me Russell had set something she'd written to music. Well, how many girls had *that* happened to? Other people got flowers, or cards or sometimes even love hearts on thin gold chains—every one of which seemed all the more unimaginative next to Jen's experience. She started arriving at school with tapes she'd borrowed from Russell stocked in her bag, and at lunchtimes, she'd hardly concentrate on what I was saying as she poured over the inlay cards. I might catch her arm to get her attention, and she'd slip her walkman headphones over my head, holding them over my ears as if she were protecting them with small black muffs. It only served to underline my exclusion. The tapes were usually of Russell's band, his voice echoey and drawn out, the words ringing as if rebounding from exposed metal pipes in an empty warehouse. She'd watch me with light skipping in her green eyes. 'Do you like it?' There was a new, unwary eagerness to her question.

Each time she tried to share, I felt second best, redundant. Even when she showed me a small, purple notebook she'd taken to carrying around—blank, unlined, hard-covered, and with her star sign printed in gold on the outside. Inside it, she wrote short, spare blocks of words: always thin. I took them, at first glance, to be lists of some sort. She told me they were song lyrics, and she wanted me to read them before she showed them to Russell. They were full of 'I' and 'you', words like 'night', 'black', 'dream', 'thorn', 'torn', 'cut'. A small part of me almost coldly winced for her.

The lyrics were strange, raw things; I wondered at the wisdom of showing them to him. But Russell liked some of her songs, she said; and it was one of these lyrics which he'd written music for, asking if Lazarus could put it on their set list. It was as if they'd begun inventing a language of their own together. I yearned to have someone think that highly of me. Of something *I'd* thought, *I'd* made.

Being so often in my room studying made me a convenient alibi for Jenny. On the rare occasions when Gerald came home early from work and asked Marion where Jenny was, he'd phone my place, and I'd tell him she was already on her way back. Then I'd call Jenny at Russell's or jump on my bicycle and sprint to his band practice rooms. Not that Gerald or Marion particularly minded her having a boyfriend. Marion seemed to have reached a point where she was simply relieved that Gerald's kids were growing up and the house was emptying out. Gareth had already left town.

'She acts like it's a huge inconvenience whenever we're in,' Jenny said. 'Like it's *such* a pain to have me and Jonathon around, when just about all she does now is slob out in front of TV. The other night, when I went to help with dinner, she said, "What are *you* doing here?" And Dad got a bit pissed off with her. "She *lives* here, Marion".' Jenny sucked in air quickly over her teeth. 'I tell you, he sure did have some making up to do after that. I had to do all the cooking while they had a row—him saying, "Don't be so sensitive, sweetheart," and her saying he took her for granted and degraded her. By the end of it, I was just about ready to climb out of the window. I'm *glad* I'm hardly ever there.'

But if Marion hardly cared about what hours Jenny kept, Gerald had sudden fatherly pangs now and then, when Jen wasn't around. He'd sound concerned when he phoned, but when Jen went home he'd never mention that he'd been worried about where she'd been. He'd just have words with her about studying harder. He had transferred on to her his hopes for one of his children to carry on in education and Gerald often announced to people that she was 'going to be a linguist, a translator'. I could hear the pride and love in his voice when he talked about Jen's future in front of us, but she could only hear him pressuring her to be his ideal.

As Jen came to our house less and less, my mother began to worry about me. She asked repeatedly if Jenny and I had argued. I kept saying 'No, I told you. Jenny is spending time with her new boyfriend.' To which she'd reply, 'Oh *dear!*' Not only had I been left on the shelf, she implied, but the shelf was dusty and inaccessible, and I'd turned into a chipped and empty jar, growing a muzzle of green mould. So I stopped saying that, and replaced it with, 'Mum, you know exams are getting closer.' And eventually, 'Would you mind just leaving me alone for a while?' As soon as I said that, Mum hit the roof. In her way. Never fireworks, like at Jenny's place: just long, probing questions.

'We've always talked about our problems, Marie. You can't bottle things up. Now, tell me what's going on. What are you being so secretive about? You're always shutting yourself away, you never spend time with me and your father. What's happening?'

'Nothing, Mum, I'm just busy.'

'You look more tired than usual. It's not like you to be this way.' She'd try to finger my hair or to drape a cardigan around my shoulders. Little bugs of disgust crept over my scalp and along my arms.

'Please, I just need some time to get through this work. *People* interfering is what's really annoying me.'

'So you *are* unhappy.'

I stood up and pulled my door right back. 'Yes, Mum, I'm unhappy—I'm trying to study, and *someone* keeps coming into my room! Now, please—'

I ended up buying a small bolted lock and putting it on my door myself so I could study in peace. Which I didn't get. Mum pushed leaflets about marijuana under my door. Is your child becoming more reclusive? they said. Are your child's eyes bloodshot? Have you noticed unusual moodswings, or a change in your child's social patterns?

I showed them to Jenny.

'Oh, Christ,' she said. 'Your Mum needs her head read. Maybe it's menopause. You should give her a leaflet on that.'

I studied even harder to get away from the nettling, and succeeded in tiring myself out by nine o'clock each night. I would ease myself into bed before ten, aching as if with influenza, my body slowly uncramping from its slouch over my textbooks. Often I would frown into the dark, thinking about Jen, and how, although I still felt myself as intertwined with her as two strands in a plait, the strands had needed to shift to make room for Russell. One night, after Dad had been pestering me too—'All this study, you don't get enough exercise, cooped up inside all day. You'll run to fat, you know!'—I lay in bed and felt thin tears squeeze themselves free, running, as if for comfort, to my lips. Punishing myself for my pettiness, I didn't wipe them away, but left them there tickling, nagging.

Though I disliked this selfish thing that had surfaced in me, the next day on the way to school I simply couldn't control it. Jenny and I were walking from her gate, where I'd picked her up, past a small park that was really no more than a duck pond and a couple of benches. Jenny asked me if I wanted to go along to a movie that weekend, and I instantly said yes.

'Oh, excellent. Russell's going to pick up the tickets beforehand, 'cause he's working, so he'll be near the theatre. He and I thought we'd get together for coffee first and then go to the film, so shall we meet you outside?'

I stopped in my tracks.

'Sometimes it feels like I'm losing you. Like you care about Russell more than me.' It leapt like a barbed fish hook, snagging at the air. Jenny stopped abruptly as well.

'What's that supposed to mean, Marie?'

'Nothing.'

'No, what do you mean?'

I watched the duck pond, the mallards with their bright jade head feathers, the ones they never seemed to shed, as if they held on to them as tightly as jewels.

'Marie?'

'I mean, it's not like we can talk the way we usually do, if he's there.' I knew that was only partly true as well; I always left as soon as I could whenever Russell arrived.

'Don't you like him?'

'It's not *that*—oh, never mind. It doesn't matter.'

'You know he likes you—he told me he thinks you have a strange way of seeing things, that he likes. That you're quiet, but he can tell you're taking it all in, thinking it through. I told him that was exactly what I'd said to you when we first became friends.' She was looking away from me, watching the pond.

'He does?' I said stupidly.

'Marie, just come to the movie. You should learn to have more fun.'

That stung. Fun was what Jenny and I had always had. Together. But Jenny had more fun with Russell than she did with me. And *he* thought I was quiet and strange.

We walked on to school in silence. I was smarting; a fresh sense of injury swept through me each time I thought over her words: 'quiet, strange, should have more fun'.

By the time we met up again in the common room at lunch time, I had managed to work myself up into thinking that the movie invitation was the most complex problem I had ever had to deal with. I didn't want to go. I didn't believe Jenny really wanted me to go. I lied to her: I told her I'd just remembered the whole family was getting together on the night of the film. 'It's so *frustrating*,' I said. 'Heather and Lucy always take over—and it's always everyone trying to talk at once, nobody getting heard.'

I slipped her a quick look. She knew I was fabricating, but she was sympathetic. We were talking in code, and the double act, the double lie, worked some combination lock, so things were free between us again. In the relief of being delivered from fighting about Russell, we were magically close-knit once more. If she had openly challenged me about making up excuses, it would have been different, but our white lies were a form of mutual care.

'Don't worry about the movie,' she said. 'Why don't you come round on Sunday afternoon instead?'

We had already planned that Sunday, which was Anzac Day, to lay our own wreath on the war memorial in the centre of town. We had decided to make a chain from any garden flowers we could find still struggling at that time of year, and to present it along with a card that said: 'Remember the dead. Forget your weapons.' We'd wondered if it might get on TV: we thought it was pretty radical. I smiled at Jen, and agreed to go round. She nudged me with her shoulder, and let it rest against me.

On Sunday we laid our shrivelling flowers, and felt shy in the crowd of elderly returned servicemen in their suits, their eyes watery with memories. We withdrew from the edges, and walked all the way back to Jen's house, trying to imagine a war, and talking about what the newspapers were saying about how a nuclear winter would affect the southern hemisphere. We talked about doing some leafleting for CND, doing something to ward off the fear in the spiky black newsprint and the perpetual foreboding in newscasters' voices. We banged into Jen's house, cheeks hot from our walk, and set to making tea and crackers with cheese, working around Gerald, who had a newspaper laid out on the kitchen bench.

'Have you read that feature about America's nuclear weapons arsenal?' I asked him, in a tone that implied any decent person would have.

'Hmmm?' He didn't look up.

'Please, can we talk about something else?' Jenny pleaded. She stacked up the snack plates on one arm, took both mugs of tea, and gestured with her head to her room, eager to get away before Gerald gave any fuller response.

As Jen tried to hustle me past the open door of the lounge, I could see Marion set up on the sofa, an ashtray on one of its arms filled with crushed cigarette stubs and crumpled Picnic bar wrappers. A cask of Montana Red and an empty wine glass sat on the coffee table in front of her as she watched the TV replay of a squash game: Susan Devoy in a match against someone who wasn't familiar to me. My sister Heather had her hair cut just like Devoy's, and talked about her as proudly as if she were a personal friend, not a compatriot: 'Susan this, Susan that . . .' As I hesitated a little in recognition, Marion felt my presence at the doorway. She looked over her shoulder, and as she moved I was already anticipating that I would read something complex on her face: excitement, passion, enthusiasm for her former sport; perhaps even regret, nostalgia, painful sentiment. But there was nothing: just a TV-drugged, indoors Sunday blank. She didn't seem to see me, just let her gaze float back to the screen. And I felt my throat constrict at the banality of it all. I pulled back from the doorway, and hurried after Jen down the corridor, shaking off the sight.

When we had arranged ourselves comfortably in Jenny's room, Jonathon popped his head around the door. It seemed ages since I'd seen him; and, as if Jenny's house were the last place I'd expect to bump into him, I gave a ridiculously surprised, 'Hello, you!' I realised how tall he had become; everything about him had thickened and filled out, even in the month or so since the senior dance.

He was in his first year of an apprenticeship at a large family-run landscape gardening business. It wasn't quite what Gerald had in mind. Jenny had told me that Jonathon loved it, though. All outdoors, and weekends off for motocross racing. He had a certain kind of woodsman's look, I thought; his freckles had nearly disappeared, his blond hair had darkened, and he'd let it grow so it was a rich tangle of curls that went past his ears. He wore a thick padded brown and white check shirt and grubby jeans, the knees lightly crusted with soil. His nails were cracked, and rimed with black; but then, they always had been, as he tinkered nearly every weekend with his bikes.

'What are you doing?' he asked.

'Just gassing.' Jenny waved a hand.

'Haven't seen you for ages,' he nodded at me.

'That's just what I was thinking,' I said.

'You're never *in*, Jon.' Jenny was trying to get rid of him.

'Speak for yourself,' he countered.

'*Bye*, Jonathon.'

'What, are you telling secrets?' He came farther into the room.

'Might be.'

'I can tell you a secret,' he teased, feigning breathless intimacy. Jenny gave him a sour look. 'Someone thinks your friend Marie's getting pretty cute.'

Jenny picked up one of her pillows and gave it to me. 'You'll need this for self-defence. He's horny.'

Jonathon's face went almost lumpy with embarrassment, and I couldn't stop myself: 'Your face has gone lumpy!' I spluttered. Jenny burst into one of her laughs, and I immediately folded the pillow over my own face, wishing I could vanish.

When I peered out, Jonathon seemed undeterred. He rocked the door on its hinges a little, running his hand along the jamb, as if checking it for rough edges, and said, 'We never go drinking in the park any more.'

I scrutinised him, to see if he was just hassling his kid sister's friend or if he remembered our playfight outside on the night Jenny and I had sneaked off to the club. And to see if, both then and now, he'd remembered that one night in the park, years ago. When his body had cupped itself towards me on the grass, and he'd asked me a slow string of questions.

'I can walk you home later, if you like.' He raked the door backwards and forwards a few more times. Jenny wolf-whistled.

'Thanks, but I'll be fine.'

He shrugged. 'I'll be around.' He closed the door after himself.

Jenny mouthed the words at me as it snicked shut, opening her lips frog-wide in mimed astonishment—OH MY GOD. I mirrored her, though I was also rather pleased. Then, before I could work out how to tell her about the time Jonathon and I had been bawled out by Marion in the back yard, Jenny went hysterical, making fun of him, and I joined her, to cover up my embarrassment. We both stood up at the door, swaggering, as we deepened our voices, raised our eyebrows and said 'looking pretty cute' over and over again.

'Looks like you've got a date,' Jenny said.

'I'll have to crawl out through the air vents!'

She drummed her fists on her thighs, laughing again, until she went floppy, and leaned against the headboard of her bed. She caught her breath, and shuffled herself over to me, hugging onto another pillow.

'I do have a secret to tell you,' she said. I wondered, for a split second, if it was about Jonathon. I nodded, but said nothing, thinking if I sounded too eager, or not interested enough, she might not tell me.

'It happened,' she said.

I knew immediately. She and Russell.

'All his flatmates were away this weekend—' We heard Jonathon walk heavily from his room to the kitchen. Jenny waited until we heard him trudge back again, and close his door. She whispered, even so. 'And we went back to his flat, after the film.'

I knew they had ended up going to an early session that Friday; I had waited with Jen outside school for Russell to come by. A girl had called back something to Jen over her shoulder as she left, and Jenny had gone over to chat to her for a moment. Russell rounded a corner and walked along the school's street, unseen by Jen. He put a finger up to his lips, motioning for me not to give him away. I watched him walk up behind her, moving nearer and leaning in, as if testing to see whether she could feel his presence, like static electricity lifting the cobweb-light down along the back of her neck and her arms. But he couldn't wait long; he murmured something in her ear, and I expected her to shy and skitter, like a startled deer, but she just cocked her head, waiting for him to finish. Her smile grew, and then slowly she faced him. I'd busied myself then, pretending to go through an exercise book I'd been carrying underneath my arm.

Jenny continued, her voice low. 'We had dinner, and we went to his room, and, you know, things just started to happen.' I wondered what things. 'And then, basically—he asked me.'

Like something long weighted to the bottom of a stream, finally dislodged by fresh, strong currents, a memory from intermediate school, form two, swam up to confuse my anticipation. Only once before had I talked properly to someone my age who said that they'd had sex. She was a girl called Tricia—*fast*, other girls said; and someone had misspelled 'Tricia is a Slut' several times in indelible marker on a concrete bus shelter near the school. Tricia had been one of a group of us playing Truth or Dare: a game suited to the restless, heedless energies of our last days at intermediate school, and to the atmosphere of intimacy and fear that had infiltrated the classroom as the last holidays before high school approached. For 'truth', Tricia said that she'd 'done it' with Paul Braithwaite, a tough thirteen-year-old we called Munt. He smoked and wore a denim jacket pockmarked with small, brown-ringed burn holes. He had what my mother called dirty-blond hair, and already a kind of cruel good looks. Tricia, who always seemed too old to be at our school, favoured close-fitting jeans, and wore blue eyeshadow that flashed like two marine flags against her enviably smooth, milk-chocolatey skin. She told the story like it was an enormous joke: how she and Munt had gone to the school playing fields late at night, and down by the cricket pitch, on the hard ground there, they'd undone their jeans together. I'd always crossed the road and pretended I hadn't seen anyone whenever Munt walked my way, and felt alarmed just hearing that Tricia had been somewhere alone with him. She rushed on with her story, saying that 'it was small, like a sausage, and it waved around so much I had to grab it to keep it still so he could get it in.' She didn't appear worried about what might happen if Munt, the tough, heard how she laughed about him, pale and wavering in the light which leaked into the school grounds.

The mixture of dread and expectation I had felt in that game of confession and humiliation echoed inside me as I waited for Jenny's account. But I couldn't help it; curiosity pressed me for more. Even if Jen hadn't been whispering, I would have; my voice had gone hoarse.

'What was it like?'

'His flat?'

'*Jenny!*'

She was thoroughly enjoying drawing it out.

'Well, the first time—'

'More than once already?'

'Do you want me to tell you or not?'

'Okay, okay.'

'The first time, Marie, I honestly thought I'd never felt anything so bad. It hurt so much, and then suddenly it was all over, and I thought, What, is that *it*? Is that what everyone makes such a fuss about? It's so stupid, but I cried. And—'

'Oh, Jenny—' I was appalled.

But Jenny's hands went up in the air to stop me continuing. 'So I just thought, That can't be right. And I told him we had to try again.'

My mouth dropped open.

Jenny cradled her pillow more closely to herself. 'Then it was like . . . it's impossible to explain.'

Her eyes searched the ceiling as if she really might not be able to carry on. I felt cold, as if I had shrunk inside my clothes, and now they were loose and outsized, letting in shivers and currents of frosty air. I could only repeat myself.

'What was it like?'

'It's like you laugh with your insides.'

'What?'

'No, it's not like that. It's like—getting a little drunk and drowning. It's like drowning and flying through warm space.'

'No. It can't be like that.'

'But it is. It's like sinking, like falling through something soft.'

'How can you be flying and falling at the same time?'

'You just—do. And do you know what? I sort of ache all over, like I've lifted something really heavy, or been on a long walk uphill. But it's actually kind of nice. Like a reminder.'

I was more nonplussed than ever. 'Weren't you nervous? Or scared?' I tried to imagine Jenny being that matter-of-fact and bold with Russell, showing the same practical determination as she did when we shut ourselves in her room with the *Cleo* magazine.

Jenny shook her head, unsmiling, although in a manner that made me feel she was accepting me into something. 'Not scared,' she said. 'I wanted to. Russell—he's just so—I really wanted to.'

'Did you use contraception?'

'Of course.'

'Condoms?'

'Yep.'

'Were they yours or his?'

'Mine. You've got to look after yourself, you know. I'm not relying on anyone else to make my decisions.'

I don't think she ever said to me, outright, that she loved him. Perhaps things moved too fast. Perhaps she would have, rolling the word over and over under her breath, if there'd been more time to think, to explore. It's a word that could have come so easily, that she could have used from the first giddy weeks—it was such common currency. A word tattooed with penknives and with red, green or blue ballpoint pen, over our desks and chairs at school, over the toilet walls, done in thick marker all over girls' canvas school-satchels. It came up in every song on the radio, was said in every film we saw. Perhaps she was waiting, making sure. Then time ran out, and there was no real point in saying it to me, to seal what was happening.

When I left Jenny's home late that afternoon, I was so preoccupied with what we had talked about that I jumped when Jonathon called my name. He jogged to catch up with me.

'Hi,' he said, unnecessarily. 'Look, I'm sorry if I embarrassed you before.'

'That's okay.'

I carried on walking, and he kept up beside me. He didn't say anything for a few seconds, then he scuffed to a stop. I waited.

'Marie, do you know very much about Russell?' He searched my face.

Cars passed regularly, as if they were measuring out the length of my pause.

'What sort of things?'

Jonathon gave a questioning gesture, and then absentmindedly ran one hand along a hedge in someone's front garden. Small red berries scrambled to the ground. 'Do you think he's okay?'

'He seems nice enough, I suppose.'

He nodded, gently sucking his lips into a thin line, pressing all the colour from them. 'He's not going to hurt her or anything, is he?'

That startled me. Had he overheard our conversation?

'What? Hurt her? Well, he's not aggressive, if that's what you're worried about.'

Jonathon's eyes followed the passage of the cars, back and forth. 'No, that's not really what I mean. I don't know. I know she's seeing a lot of him, that's all.'

His tone was oddly paternal, and I had a sudden hunch. 'Has Gerald said something?'

Jonathon glanced at me. 'Not really. As long as her grades stay okay.' He gave a skewed smile. 'You know, I don't think I've ever been past your place,' he said, and gestured with his elbow to suggest that we walk on.

I tried to pick up the thread again. 'Are you really worried about Russell?'

'Curious, I guess.'

It seemed a long way to take curiosity, walking all the way home with me. 'I honestly think Jenny knows what she's doing,' I said. 'She's pretty street-wise.'

He laughed, instantly unburdened. 'You can say that again. And street's better than home, really. I don't know, maybe that's why I wanted to ask about Russell. Jenny's not exactly going to come home to talk about things, is she?'

It was an unfamiliar feeling, being invited in like this by Jonathon. 'I guess not,' I said quietly.

I stopped as we reached my driveway, the windows of our big white house shielded from the road by a low, white-painted concrete wall and huge olearia hedge that rustled as a starling searched about for some mislaid detail in its crinkled, papery leaves.

'You're good for her, though.' Jonathon stood, head down, hands plunged into his pockets and his legs straddled just the way Jenny's had the first time I saw her. 'You're kind of calm.'

I felt the blood rush to my cheeks in instant denial; it was simply that my habitual loss-for-words reinforced the impression of composure. Jonathon freed one of his hands and gripped me quickly on the upper arm. 'You look out for her,' he said.

Why did people have to do things sideways? Like Gerald

not just telling Jen he loved her but always pushing his hopes for her in the way.

'Have you talked to Jenny herself?' I asked.

'Kind of. But I wanted to know what you thought, that's all.'

It seemed he'd run out of things to say, and as we stood together I noticed the dusk: the last of the daylight must have gradually dispersed while we were talking. I tested the silence—asking him something to keep us there a little longer, curious about the novelty of being alone with him, without him lightly joshing or sloping off at the first opportunity, as if girls were an uncomfortable authority that he'd rather escape, unnoticed, unquestioned.

'Sooo—' I drew it out, watching him to see if he'd pull himself up and say he should be getting back. 'How's your new job, anyway? It must be good to be out of school.'

'Yeah, too right. Great having money—pays for the bikes and scuba diving. I'm saving up for a trip somewhere, maybe Australia—the Great Barrier Reef. Should be good.'

He didn't move, but he didn't ask me anything, either. It was as if I had to play on both sides of the net, and rush around before we were left gawping at each other in the dark.

'Have you heard from Gareth since he left?' I knew Jonathon and Jenny had received a letter: surely he'd find something to say about that.

'Yeah, yeah. Had a letter. Hasn't found a job yet, but he's all right for a while—staying with one of our aunts till things work out. You know Gareth, nothing much worries him.'

'Except Marion.'

I wished I hadn't said it. His mouth gave an uncomfortable, screwed-up look, as if talking about her left a bitter, residual paste that changed the savour of everything else afterwards.

Jonathon scanned the sky: its soupy grey upturned bowl. 'Looking forward to getting away myself,' he said. 'Hope I'll still be able to afford the scuba dive if I move out. A mate of mine's got a place, though, and I might be able to move in if he can get rid of one of his flatmates.'

I thought about leaving home. It still gave me a buzzing, airless feeling, somewhere between panic and joy. Like looking down from a high, sturdy tree branch into the best swimming hole in a river before the first jump of summer. Watching thin-limbed, supple boys scramble up and bicycle wildly in the air, whooping, before they sent up spray in flaring crowns from the spot where they plummeted through the surface, lost for terrible seconds to the green, watery caverns before they came shooting free again, shaking dark wet hair out of their eyes. And as I watched, I wanted to go in so badly—but was held back, waiting. I'd leap when everything reached a focus, the shimmering on the water somehow held for a moment, like a target.

I waited in that breathlessness—but then a thought pushed away the anticipation. 'Does all this mean you'll be leaving home before Jenny?'

Jonathon watched me, his eyebrows pulled into a small frown. 'Maybe.'

I let this sink in. A stone slowly turning, end on end, down through the layers of the swimming hole. I understood now why he'd walked me home, why he wanted to check up on Russell. Jenny would be alone more once he'd gone, and he wanted to feel able to leave—to know there would be other buffers once he'd moved out. I tried to think how it would be for Jen without either of her brothers at home, briefly reassuring myself it would only be for the rest of this year, before she came to university with me, and the boys hadn't been around much anyway. But maybe Jonathon's questions revealed something: his careful watching from the corners. And now he wanted to leave; to get away from old responsibility, to make himself anew.

My expression must have shown something of my uncertainty, for Jonathon's voice was appeasing, as if I might have been Jenny. 'I'm not going far yet. I'll still be in town.'

I nodded. It had grown much darker, and the shadows and hollows in his face seemed different, as if watching him at night were more intimate. It felt comfortable now, just standing with him. More like the times in the park when all four of us had been easy and talking, the moonlight rubbing gently into our skin and muscles. But for some reason, I pulled myself back.

'I'd better get going,' I said. 'I don't want to keep you out here.'

'Okay,' he said, and it was barely audible, as if there were someone nearby that he didn't want to wake. He stepped towards me, and dry as the touch of a leaf blown up from the ground, his lips moved quickly over my cheek. I was so surprised, I laughed. I looked down at my feet, but then he tilted my chin, and his quick, dry touch passed again over my mouth. I was immediately worried that someone might see us: my father coming home early, the car headlights blazing over us; my mother misinterpreting it all and wanting to know, second by second, what had gone on; even Jenny, unpredictably deciding to visit, even though we'd had all day together. But I smiled at Jonathon, as if he must understand the irony of us standing there together—knowing each other, hardly knowing each other: the natural unnaturalness of Jenny's best friend and brother watching each other in the dark.

His hands went to my shoulders, lightly perching there, questioning. Then he fingered along my back. He closed his eyes, and now his lips felt full and hot, as he pressed with more conviction. The tip of his tongue licked at me, tentative and exploring. I felt a warm rushing, and opened my mouth blindly ... then doubt clambered all over me, everything was ruined: it was all suddenly too much, like being fed a cold fish belly. I pulled away, my hands up on his chest.

'Jonathon, this isn't right. I should go inside.'

He leaned back, as though trying to see me more clearly. 'Are you sure?' he said.

I wasn't one hundred percent certain. I'd have quite liked to rewind a little, to the new surprise of his first kiss, and hold it there, for hours even. But then what? Jonathon was Jenny's brother. The night air closed in; the town could catch me and keep me in it for ever if I wasn't careful. I breathed in.

'I'm sure.'

I wasn't at all afraid of hurting him. This was happening in a separate space, a place that would vanish by morning. It was like the wavering, uncertain landscape seen from a car in a heatwave: there, and then not there, as you drive onwards, everything ahead turning solid upon your approach.

'Okay,' he said. And his tone said he'd seen what I'd seen. 'You be good.' He turned to walk away. 'See you round.'

It was over. I ran up the driveway, speeding on relief and a separate, secret satisfaction. *I had been kissed.*

I never told Jenny about that encounter. I wanted to, to go carefully over the mystery of it all, unravelling a complicated back route on a road map. How I wished it had been someone else! But it remained an unspoken pact between us. When I came across Jonathon now and then, outside Jenny's gate, arriving or leaving her house, we were cheerful and friendly in our hellos and small-talk. If I was ever melancholy or anxious when we met, those feelings would instantly crumble and scatter. 'A soft spot,' I thought. 'I have a soft spot for Jonathon.' But I also read the slow crinkling at the sides of his eyes as a sign of what we knew together, silently. We were sparing each other the trickiness of exposure. The scene was something we'd tried once, and not taken up. That was all.

Yet from that night I had learnt that my instinct about the separateness of what went on between two people was right. There were some things you held tightly to yourself: away even from your best friend. Which was why, when Jenny confided in me later, well before Russell, my shock was accompanied by a sense of special privilege.

It was in the middle of June, just before our mock exams, when in an experiment initiated by the seventh form dean, the seniors were given one week's study leave in the lead-up to the internal exams. Not even I could study for fourteen hours a day, so Jenny and I got to see more of each other while Russell was at work. One us would get fed up with solitary book confinement, and phone up the other to suggest a walk, a coffee or perhaps a study session together.

Some time during that week Jenny told me that Blake had finally left town. So what? I thought. Suited me. Like Catherine in the orange jersey and tartan skirt, playing on the bars when I was six, he had gone: stopped. And I never asked after him again. Now these exits puzzle me, knowing what I do about Jen. People just leave, then day and night flood in, time emptying into their places like water resettling after a swimmer has climbed free, streams of it rushing from the skin, back to its source.

One afternoon, the winds high, Jenny and I asked my mother, who was working a half day, to drop us off along the coast for a walk. The waves were fierce, but we needed the weather's assault. The rimey spray and the wind that carried flecks of shell and sand scrubbed us clean of the smothering feeling that the approach of exams gave us. It drove us closer together, for warmth, and to stop our words from whipping away from us as we walked. But we didn't last for long on that wild coast: Jenny seemed to tire quickly, and she clung to me now and then when rocks came loose as we stepped along them or when the battle against the wind unbalanced us.

We ended up walking arm in arm all the way back to the bus stop—the one where she'd driven away from me once: the last before the coastal highway began and where out-of-town bus trips felt as if they really started. Later, back in our favourite café, I ordered a coffee but Jenny had, unusually, decided on Earl Grey tea. As we reached our seats, the way she sat down gingerly, took one minute sip, and then pushed the teacup away with an uncomfortable stretch of her arm made me ask her if everything was all right. Her skin looked odd, ashen.

'I don't know,' she said. 'I've been feeling pretty queasy for the past week . . . .' She trailed off, examining her fingernails, and I guessed straight away what was wrong. I said nothing. 'There's always a taste of oranges in my mouth—oranges.' She looked distractedly at someone passing by the table, then she leaned her forehead in the palm of one hand.

'Do you need to go to the bathroom?'

I moved our bags in case she had to hurry, but, rubbing her forehead against her hand, she shook her head. 'No, I don't want to move. I just need to sit still. Do you mind if we stay here for a while? You don't have to go anywhere, do you?'

Her large green eyes stayed cast down at the table top where she began to turn her saucer around and around. I decided to confront her.

'Jenny, have you missed your period?'

Her head stayed down. She nodded. 'I can't stand even the *smell* of all my favourite foods—fried onions, fresh coffee. It all gives me the same terrible taste of oranges in my mouth.'

I couldn't think clearly, just let my confirmed guess wash over me more fully. 'Oh shit,' I said. 'Shit.'

Her hand sprang from her brow and she shot out: 'What, Marie? What? What's wrong with it? Did I say there was anything wrong with it? Did I say it was bad? Have you asked me what I think yet?'

I felt heat flood my cheeks and I faltered. 'No, no, I'm sorry, Jen, it's just such a shock—I mean, it can be a good shock, if you're happy, but you seem . . .'

'Yeah, well I am. I *am*, okay? I am happy.'

She fell to toying with her saucer again, and a few seconds later, I found myself copying her in a nervous gesture of reconciliation. Our china clinked, like quietly ticking clocks. I shuffled in my seat.

'I'm sorry,' I said again, and again she started up:

'You know, Marie, just because it's not something you'd want, it doesn't mean I mightn't want it. We are two different people. We have separate lives.'

I frowned down into my coffee.

'It's okay,' she said, as an afterthought, as if she'd only just caught up with my second apology. 'But I've decided I am going to have the baby. I haven't told Russell yet—' I looked up with a jerk of disbelief—'but I'm sure he'll be happy . . .'

This was ridiculous! Why did she have to jump all the time, jump into the unknown, the fraught, the least likely situation? She'd only been with Russell for about four months. Four months! Christ, she was so young—and Gerald and Marion wouldn't allow it—where would she live? Was Russell's wage enough to support a baby? Was this really Jenny, the same person I'd always seen so high on adventure? Questions swirled in my head, but my face must have retained its look of incredulity, because Jenny straightened in her seat, as if a rigid posture could add conviction.

'If he's upset,' she began, 'I'll think again. But I think he'll go with whatever decision I want to make. And it'll be easy together. I'll be able to leave home in a year or so.' What? A *year*? 'We'd only be waiting for him to get enough of a pay rise—he's paid youth rates at the moment, but he's twenty at the end of the year, and there are assessments at the store coming up, and he might get a promotion . . .' Jenny hurried on, tumbling one explanation over another.

She sounded like someone completely different. As though she'd aged overnight. She was trying to explain how she could have the baby, but there was something wrong. She was talking about staying here—with Russell.

Whenever we'd dreamed up our plans for leaving town, it had been a given that we'd be together. We'd even agreed we'd be travelling companions after university. I had so many images of us together: on trains, feet up on the opposite seats, bulging bags on the floor, watching green fields flicker by, or standing in a city centre with packs, caps and maps, deciding on a direction, maybe kicking our way through a park scattered with scarlet leaves. Or running down a white beach to an electric-blue sea, watching the waves again. But she was staying here. Greysville. Flatsville. Dead-end-streets-ville. It seemed impossible precisely because it couldn't include me.

I asked Jenny again if she was sure she wanted to have the baby, and her face looked as if she were fighting to protect some thought, wished I would just be quiet. Now, when I remember her reluctance to answer me in that moment, I think she avoided it because she was afraid, at that early stage, to make a decision, to take action instead of just letting things happen. It was far easier for her to live day by day, as usual.

I didn't of course witness the scenes where she told Russell, or her family, but I made Jen go through it all for me afterwards. She told me that Russell's reaction, at first, was pale astonishment. He kept saying, 'Are you sure? Are you sure?' As if what they had done couldn't possibly have such a consequence.

'I got so frustrated with him,' she said. Apparently they quarrelled. He stood up, and she started to cry. She thought he was going to walk out. He sat again, bewildered, she said, like a little boy who'd woken up in a strange room and couldn't remember why he was there. Soon Jenny's crying broke through his stupor, and he held her, rocking her, until she could talk again. She told me they spent hours going over and over what they would have to do, until he reached a gradual, thawing acceptance. By the time they confronted Marion and Gerald, he presented steady dedication to the idea—to them at least.

'Underneath, I'm not really sure what he thinks,' she said, and looked at the lines in the palms of one hand, as if trying to locate some small, muscular pain that beat there. 'I'm not convinced he's happy. Like you said.'

I try to imagine Russell's face when she told him, and for the first time I can understand how powerless he must have felt. How unreal it must have seemed to him to have such a situation result so soon, from such beginnings. The lightness of dancing. Bruised lyrics in fountain pen on marbled blue paper. Night Queen incense, and thick white candles bought at the local Catholic Supplies shop. Stretching himself the length of her, weighting down her body, like paper under stone . . . holding her steady like something he didn't want to lose, something that could be lifted and carried away by the next breeze. All the self-created mysteries of two people in a rented room, marks on walls hidden beneath postcards, band posters, newspaper photos. All the intrigue to end in this: the blunt fact. The most likely of unlikely outcomes.

I can see Jenny again, as she confessed it all to me, her eyes darkening. 'Having him there, helping—that's better than nothing, isn't it?'

Even then, she didn't mention love, and I didn't ask. Instead, I focused on what I thought would be her real problems.

'What about your parents?'

Apparently, Marion and Gerald had raised an even longer list of objections than the one I had heard in my head. 'I was absolutely shitting myself before I told them,' Jen answered. 'Absolutely shitting.'

I swallowed, hands balled in my lap, thinking of what she'd told me about Marion's miscarriages. For a moment I could hardly bear to know how she'd reacted.

Jenny exhaled wearily. 'Marion even looked upset,' she said. 'I guess she doesn't think it's fair.' And Gerald had rubbed at his neck, then asked if Jenny had considered adoption: 'It's the most sensible suggestion. We could organise it for you.'

'I told them, it's *my* baby,' Jenny said, and she told me that Russell had stayed her, his arm around her waist. After half an hour of raised voices, he offered them a bottle of sparkling wine he had brought, insistent that this should be a celebration. A few glasses on, although Marion was still objecting, Jenny said that Gerald 'just seemed to change his mind'. That strikes me as particularly unusual now, but at the time it was odd only in the way of all Gerald's sudden twists of allegiance between Marion and his children.

'Dad got all emotional, and said we'd just have to bring the baby home for the first year, while Russell saves and works himself up to the promotion,' Jenny told me. Russell had found out he wasn't to receive anything in the current pay review, simply because he was too young, according to his boss, 'and might fly off any minute to better things'. Russell said he only had a thousand dollars in savings. 'Enough for a couple of honeymoon tickets to Australia,' he'd joked to Gerald and Marion, 'but not enough to buy a house.'

Russell's accommodation was a tiny room in a ramshackle house that Jenny said grew exotic kinds of mildew everywhere. 'I saw some kind of long mushroom thing coming out of wet sheets that someone had left dumped on the laundry floor,' she told me, screwing up her nose. 'You could get really sick there, I reckon.'

Watching Jenny's face, to see how she'd come through it all, I could see only relief, as if an argument were over at last, and she didn't have to consider how anyone else felt about it any more.

So it was no fairy tale, but neither was it the instant tragedy I'd expected it to be. Jenny even carried on at our school— Gerald had insisted on that—but she was happy to. 'I've got nothing to hide,' she said to me, when I asked if she was nervous about what people would say. 'What's wrong with what I've done?'

Gerald, Jenny and Russell did have a meeting with our headmistress, though, and told her that Jen and Russell were engaged. So people soon found out, though the pregnancy wasn't obvious until the last couple of months. There was some whispering in the common room, but Jenny wouldn't stand for it. Once, when a tight knot of girls stopped talking and watched her when she came into the room, she went over and asked if any of them would like to feel the baby kick. After that she was like a seventh form mascot: everyone wanted to sit with her, ask her questions about how she was feeling, what it was like, or talk about what their mothers had said about their pregnancies.

As Jenny's pregnancy went on, I began to acknowledge that she would one day move in with Russell, and be a mother just before she turned eighteen. And to my surprise, I too began to love learning all the tiny details about how she felt: what she could and couldn't eat; how her breasts had grown and felt as tender as a thin-skinned fruit about to burst and deposit thick seeds; what the doctor had said; what baby clothes she was looking for (still at the second-hand shops). And I began to ponder on what kind of gift I could give them both. I figured it needed to be important, as I was practically the baby's family, and certainly the only support Jenny had from another woman. Marion had all but stopped speaking to her.

'It's like she takes the pregnancy as a personal insult,' Jen said. 'Like I've done it deliberately. Oh yeah, right, like I'd really get pregnant just to get at her. Why can't she and Dad just be happy for me for once?'

I wanted whatever I gave Jenny to be the best, the favourite, something the baby would grow up with and remember. I asked my mother to help me sew a toy bear.

When I had first plucked up the courage to tell her about Jenny, Mum had fallen stock-still, stunned for a moment halfway across the kitchen, a colander clutched in both hands. Then she asked me questions, slowly and carefully. But when she heard that Jen wasn't going to be abandoned by Russell and hadn't dropped out of school, she started to move around from sink to bench again, absorbing it all. She appeared resigned and accepting. As if she'd known all along that something like this was likely to happen somewhere in our world; and that was precisely why she had always counselled me and my sisters so persistently.

But my father, he was different. He called me to him, alone. My recognition of him as the one who had the last word, the one who became the real disciplinarian during any family crisis, filled me with unhappy apprehension.

He stood with his hands behind his back, cleared his throat, brought one hand forward, then put it behind his back again, as if he'd just pressed Detonate.

'You will know that for some time I have thought your friendship with Jenny has been—a—a difficult subject.'

I knew no such thing. Immediately, my eyes burned as if Jenny could hear.

'She's a troubled young woman,' he continued. 'Your mother and I have been pretty hands-off until now, knowing you're a sensible girl. We've let Jenny practically live here at times, with no comment, happy to give her some sense of a welcoming home. But I'm concerned about how you're viewing this... pregnancy. It is not a thing to be admired, you know.'

I stared at him as if he were a man I barely knew. I felt betrayed. Livid. At his underestimation of me, and of my friendship. At myself, for parroting attitudes just like his when I first knew Jenny was pregnant. I took a deep breath. I didn't explode.

'What are you trying to say? Are you saying that for all these years you've never even liked her, that after all this time you don't think we should help her?'

'No, no, I'm not saying any of that. I'm not laying down any laws here, Marie, I'm simply—'

'What are you trying to tell me?' (Calm, stay calm.) Did he think that Jenny's family was going to change overnight, that suddenly she wouldn't need my support?

'What I'm trying to *ask* is whether you think your deep involvement with her at this point really is the best thing for you.'

There was no delay in my reply, although he hardly deserved one. 'The best thing for me? Yes, she is. I think she is the best thing for me. The *best thing*. I'm her *best friend*. I'd help her no matter what kind of trouble she was in. And she'd do the same for me.'

We stared at each other. Then, cautiously, I turned, half expecting him to order me back to his heels. Master and dog. But I walked away.

Mum was hovering in the kitchen, her expression controlled. So, they'd had one of their consultations. She'd known what he was going to say, but hadn't been able—or hadn't bothered—to stop him.

I tried to lunge past as she reached out to hold me.

'How can you love him?' I tore free, and went straight to my room, where I drew the curtains and flung myself on my bed, as if I could bury myself in the dark, or at least make her think I was asleep. I knew she would come to me later.

When she did, she knocked softly, and stood there, a dim shape.

'Your father's sorry for what he said,' she whispered. 'He knows he over-reacted.'

I didn't reply. She must have known how it weakened his apology, sending her in as his envoy.

That day undermined the closeness I had achieved with my father over the preceding summer. It shifted things a little between me and my mother, as well. There was an extra caution, I suppose, as I came to see her as more in league with Dad than her initial response to Jenny had indicated. At least the wariness meant she showed a new respect for me. I could feel her trying to edge towards me again, as she offered me tips to pass on to Jen and asked after her every single day. And she did help me to sew a yellow Pooh bear for the baby. I realised, when I got it home, that the fur I'd chosen resembled Russell's velveteen crop.

One weekend afternoon, I got a call from Jenny. 'I'm coming round,' she said, and hung up immediately. Her manner made me anxious, so I jumped on my bicycle to meet her en route. I was right: I knew something was wrong as soon as I saw her. Her face was swollen with crying. Little tracks of the tinted mascara she'd taken to wearing ran below her eyes in small blue tributaries.

'Bitch. Bitch bitch bitch. Fucking fucking bitch.'

Marion.

'What did she do?' I tried to wheel my bike and keep one arm around Jen at the same time.

'She's never asked how I'm feeling, or what the pregnancy's like—she never even *speaks* to me any more. I mean, she's never even given me a chance. You'd think this would make a difference, that she'd see me as an adult. God, even *want* to talk to me about her own experiences. But she hates me. She hates everything about me. I bet she even hates the baby already, just because it's mine . . . .' I tugged Jenny closer to me for a quick moment, reining her in, trying to stop her from thinking such things. She protested. 'Honestly, Marie, it's true, she blanks me all the time. She's walked right out of the room when I've walked in. And Dad doesn't even comment. Wants a *quiet* life.' Jenny's voice thinned. 'I heard her on the phone yesterday. She did it deliberately. She was talking to a friend about adoptions again. Right in front of me. When I walked past, she raised her voice and looked right at me. Bloody bloody *bitch*.' She dug with her knuckles at the tears that jumped up again, stubborn weeds. 'It's not like I don't need their help at the moment. Do they think this is so easy?'

'Jen,' I said, 'don't let Marion get to you like that. If she gets to you, she's won. She's only trying to upset you.'

'What do you mean, *only* trying to upset me? Isn't that bad enough?'

I tried again. 'She's envious—envious of you and Russell, jealous you're going to get away and have your own life eventually. And your Dad—' (I felt my own inadequacy here) 'he, well, maybe he just doesn't know what to say. You know what he's like. But you can't let them make you cry any more, Jen, you're not the little kid Marion thinks you are. Look!' I poked her, gently, in the stomach. 'You're almost a mum!'

She gave me a big, wet look. 'I'm going to be a terrible mum.'

'What do you mean?'

'Still burst into tears all the time, don't I?'

'Jenny. The Pope would burst into tears if he had to live with Marion.'

She choked, half-sob, half-laugh. I dug around in my jeans pockets, and came up with a clump of tissue that had gone through the wash. 'Here.'

She took my offering, but held it in one fist. 'How am I going to know how to bring up any baby if all I have to go by is Marion?'

'You'll know how not to do it, won't you? Plus you're ten times more intelligent than her to begin with.'

She looked away from me. 'Pretty dumb getting pregnant. I knew about the morning-after pill. But when the condom burst, I just thought that at that time of the month it would be okay.'

'Jenny.' I stopped. 'You do still want the baby, don't you? Isn't that why you were upset about Marion?'

She watched the pavement.

'Jen?' I didn't like this confused, stumbling feeling. 'Jen?'

She looked up at last. 'Yeah.'

We walked on. Hormones, I thought. In one of her attempts to patch things up with me again, Mum had told me all about how Jenny might get moodswings, because of hormones. When I remembered that, the pavement and sky stopped their awful teetering.

'Jen, you'll be okay. You're probably so affected by Marion because of what's happening to your body at the moment, you know, your hormones are probably in chaos. You should cry all you want.'

'Yeah?'

'Yeah.'

'Pretty wicked ones.'

We'd reached a busy intersection. Heavily and deliberately, she walked out in front of the traffic. 'This is a pedestrian crossing!' she yelled at one car. 'And I'm a pregnant woman, with wicked hormones!'

'Jenny!' I caught up with her and shepherded her off the road. She laughed, giddy.

'Stupid bitch,' she said. I wasn't sure if she meant her, me or Marion. But I took the tissues out of her fist and mopped at the blue trickles. 'You look like you're crying felt pen.'

She punched me in the arm, a little harder than I thought was necessary. Obviously still wound up. I decided silence was probably the best policy, until she was ready to talk again.

When we got to my place, I ushered Jenny around the side, so that I could put away my bike and, I hoped, avoid my father by using the back entrance. But as I opened the door, Dad was heading down the back hall to the rear cupboard, packs of batteries in his hands. He was monitoring all the family's earthquake supplies, replacing the spare batteries for the torches and radios: his six-monthly ritual. It probably seemed completely innocuous to Jenny, but I felt myself prickle with irritation. Jenny knew nothing of my altercation with him, and she tried to summon up some sparkle.

'Hi there, Mr Conway!' Her face was still hayfever puffy with crying. I put my hand in the small of her back to urge her past him. I stared him in the eye, daring him to show that he thought her blotchiness was more evidence of how 'troubled' she was.

'Jenny,' he greeted, but his tone sounded as if he were testing her name, doubtful that this pregnant teenager could be who he thought she was.

I pushed Jenny a little. She looked over her shoulder at me. I pushed her again, and I saw comprehension tug at the little lines of her face. Head down, she moved quickly to my room. I felt the cool trail of air we left behind us. I closed and bolted my door.

'What's up with your Dad?' she asked.

'He's being a complete wanker.' I kept my voice down. 'Christ, I mean, it's only a couple of months till I'm out of this town, and he's not bloody doing anything to make me want to stay.'

Jenny lowered herself onto my bed, and I fluffed up pillows for her. 'I know what you mean,' she said. 'Sometimes, I could kick myself. I can't believe I'll still have to live at home after the baby's born. If they're practically ignoring me now, how are they going to be when it's arrived?'

'I wish I could have you stay here, with my folks,' I said. My room, and of course my sisters' old rooms, would all be empty when I was at university. I was sure my mother would agree if I explained, but my father . . .

Jenny read my expression. 'They wouldn't know how to cope with it, Marie. I'm someone else's disappointment.'

'Don't talk like that.'

'It's true. I'm not their problem.' She looked around my room, as though trying to take some measure of me and this was the first time she'd seen my surroundings. She sighed. 'Sometimes I get so panicky about the future. I wish I could know it would all turn out okay. In the end. I don't even have to know *what* happens, exactly: just if somehow, someone could tell me it will all be all right. Do you know what I mean?'

'You mean the birth?'

'Everything.' Her eyes searched out through my window, scanning the framed piece of sky, white with cloud that afternoon. 'I've never been completely free. Completely. You're going to love getting away to university. I really envy you.'

I laughed. 'You envy me? That sounds so strange.' A little rock of embarrassment rolled in front of my words, making it difficult to speak. 'I've always envied you. Your looks, your courage. Your boyfriend.'

'Huh.' Jenny pressed a hand to one side of her belly, and smiled, gazing off through the window again. 'Marie, do you want to know a terrible thing?'

I didn't answer.

'When I think about what it will be like in ten years, I don't think about us. Me and Russell, I mean. I still imagine all the things you and I have talked about. Learning languages, travelling, working. Then I have to remind myself. "Wait, stop, it's all different now. It's not just me that I have to think about." But it doesn't seem real.' Involuntarily, I looked at the hand on Jen's belly. She coloured slightly. 'I know this is real,' she said. 'But ten years from now—I can't picture it. Is it all really going to carry on? Oh, I'm not explaining properly.'

'Yes, you are,' I said, so that she would continue.

'I look at Russell, and I feel lucky that he's stuck around. Amazed that he's stuck around. But then, as soon as I realise that I'm amazed, I panic. I think, is something not right about us? Why should I be amazed? Does it mean that underneath I don't expect this all to work?'

I remembered her determination in the café when she first told me she was pregnant, and for a moment I was angry at her for not feeling these things earlier, or for feeling them at all. What about how transfixed she and Russell had been with each other? Why couldn't she be consistent? I didn't know where to put my support, was being tugged from one opinion to the other. I wanted to help, but was afraid of saying the wrong thing.

'Sometimes I just wish someone I trusted could make the decisions for me,' Jen said. 'Say, "*This* is the best decision, your life will be straight after this."'

I chewed my lip. 'But that wouldn't be real freedom.'

She angled her head to one side. 'No. I guess not.'

Then quickly, her face changed and she took my hand. 'Feel. Can you feel?' she asked.

Beneath my palm, the baby, tumbling.

Jenny and I went to sit our school exams side by side. She was about seven months' pregnant, and a bit more philosophical about them than I; I behaved as if my whole life depended on them. I was desperate to do well, to earn a bursary and ensure a place at university.

When the last exam was over, the stress left me like air from a tyre. I dropped my pen, fell back in my chair, and Jenny leaned across. Her arms went around me, and I could feel her stomach pressing against my side as we rocked backwards and forwards in front of the exam steward: the same supervisor I'd had for my School Certificate exams, and whose skill at handicrafts I had learned to dread. She was a squat, white-haired woman who with clacking metallic needles knitted incessantly throughout most of our papers. As Jenny and I gave small cries of 'It's all over!', she came up behind us and struck me on the shoulder with her knitting needles. I pulled away, about to tell her to 'bugger off,' when she presented Jenny with four pairs of woollen booties done in white, three shades of blue, and even black: the school colours. The expression on Jenny's face was unforgettable: overcome and radiant; overcome with radiance. I grinned at the examiner and forgave her the hours of tormenting clicking.

Then we were at liberty for the whole summer. Very grudgingly, I had asked Dad for work at the local supermarket again, to sustain my savings, but I was otherwise free just to wait for the baby, and for February, when I would be moving away. Jenny and I hadn't really talked about what that separation would be like: I simply assumed I would come back whenever I could, just to see her.

The last few weeks of Jen's pregnancy seemed to move more slowly than the weeks before exams. The days oozed like syrup, heavy and sleepy, and each stroke of every second was like a separate testing instrument pressing on the strong, taut outside of Jenny's stomach, and listening, listening, for a reaction. We were tense and alert. I say we: obviously it must have been worse for Russell, but I'm ashamed of how few memories I have of him from this time. I still wanted to think of Jenny and I as the double-barrel we had been: JennyandMarie. Though the evidence would always be right in front of me, it was possible for me to believe this was Jenny's pregnancy, alone, and it was me she really needed to talk with about whether or not she was comfortable, whether or not she was all right doing everything from drinking coffee to swimming . . .

These memories may be coloured by hindsight: by my efforts to find answers to the worst of all unsolved questions, to hunt down patterns and hints in the prelude. (But what else could anyone do with a haunting like this? I have heard of families who keep whole rooms the same; who set an extra place at the table that stays empty for years and years, because they can't find an answer, because there isn't one solid fact that they can accept as proof. The people who are left behind are the ones who get no rest. Their voices are the ones that moan through the trees and freeze hallways . . .) Yet I do feel that as the day got closer, Jenny became more and more anxious, a grey shadow fleeting over her face now and then, an invisible hand passing over her eyes, measuring her vision, her reactions. A shadow of what? I tried to stay with her as much as I could, as often as my job would let me.

Jenny's baby didn't know that I considered myself her watchguard. On the last day of January, a skin-scorching day, it chose to turn, kick and push within Jen as she swam down at the beach—our beach—with Russell and Jonathon. Russell had taken a few extra days off in anticipation of the birth, and Jonathon, finishing work early, offered to drive them down to the coast; he seemed to be trying to get to know Russell a little more. He told me later that Jenny had insisted on going into the water, promising she just wanted to cool off. All three of them waded in up to their waists, and she floated in Russell's arms as he lifted her up with each wave—until a large, glassy-green wall rose in front of them and collapsed. They came up, gasping, Jenny shaking the fringed and beaded shawl of water from her hair and eyes. She slipped away from Russell, singing out, 'Silly prick!' and ducked her head again as he tried to swim after her. She sidestroked, watching him and laughing as he called out to her. As she kicked, her belly began to give intense, seizing contractions that moved right through to her back. Jonathon told me later that he knew immediately, from the way 'Jenny's face—sort of—stopped.' He and Russell swam to her, each put an arm around her, and paddled, bodysurfed, stumbled to shore.

Jonathon was the one who called me. They managed to get to the hospital, and the baby arrived on the very day predicted. Everyone had thought that so unlikely, it felt like a dramatic change of plan. I was so excited I forgot to tell Jonathon to congratulate Russell: just rushed on to questions about Jenny, and Chrissy, the little girl. Jonathon told me that I must go and see her as soon as I could, but the next morning at the earliest, as now they were both sleeping. I longed to see them both that instant, but I thanked him for calling me so soon. 'You're an uncle!' I said to him.

He sounded taken aback. 'Yeah. Wow. An uncle.'

I laughed, said goodbye, but didn't hear him respond. As I put the phone down, I imagined him still sitting there, listening to the reverberations of his new role.

And then, things sped up. Events rocketed, faster and faster, like a spool of film spun forward, images jerking and tumbling over each other, racing beyond the point at which, now, I wish I could hold them. The sharp, clattering sound of the end of the reel, the acrid scent of a bulb burning out: I want to stop the memories from moving this quickly, although they are struggling to keep up with the rate at which events happened. If only I could slow them down and find some detail I've missed before—a figure in the background or a word, a moment between us that I could enlarge and examine, use to solve everything. Resolve everything. Dissolve the ache that sits deep at the back of my throat when I think about Jenny, or Chrissy, or having my own children. An ache that means it would hurt to speak, that the cells of our bodies remember when we lose someone. Our tongues know they've been cut to stumps, they know they will have to relearn how to say the names of those we've lost.

I did go to see Jenny and the baby the next day. Red as a kidney bean, and curled up as tightly, Chrissy slept with her whole fist in her mouth. The sight of her entered me with silent footfall. The weirdest, most wonderful feeling. Months of waiting, and still she took my breath away, as if I hadn't fully registered that a real baby, a new person entirely in her own right, was who we were expecting.

Jenny was exhausted, and tears leaked from her like her milk as we hugged. I asked her if she was happy, and she looked across at where Chrissy slept. In answer, she told me that she had just finished a difficult visit from Marion and Gerald, but (and I cursed myself for it later) I tried to brush it off. Keep Jen going, I thought. Keep her up, keep her happy, it's not good to let her dwell on those two. And—oh, so selfishly—I just wanted to look at Chrissy.

'Marion's jealous,' I said, my standard line. 'Who cares? You'll be away eventually.' Jenny smiled uncertainly, and pulled me down into her arms again. She shook a little, and I was needled by confusion. I wanted her to be happy; I'd expected her to be happy. I tried to distract her.

'Look at your daughter,' I said. Jen looked. 'Jen, can I wake her up, please? Can I hold her?'

She plucked at the bed covers. 'I don't know. I don't know if the nurses would say if you should.'

'Oh, come on, Jen, you're the mother. You'll let me, won't you?'

She didn't say no. I went over to the crib, and got my hands into the soft layers of baby linen. Frightened that I would hurt her, I picked up this tiny thing, this solid, living Chrissy. I pressed my nose against the baby's delicate head as I kissed her, and took in her smell. What was it like?

'Chrissy girl,' I said. 'Little Chrissy girl.' I took her over to Jenny's bed. 'There's your Mum.' Chrissy was barely awake, but her mouth tasted at the air. 'Smell her, Jen. How would you describe it?'

Jenny breathed in. 'Hospitals. I can only smell hospital.'

'Do you want to hold her?' I asked, though I didn't want to give her up.

'No, that's okay,' she answered. 'You can have a long go.' She looked at the baby solemnly. I wondered if she was annoyed that I'd picked her up: maybe she'd only just gone off to sleep when I arrived.

I kissed Chrissy on the forehead again, and with a feeling that something was being pulled away from me, I put her back into the crib, making sure all the blankets were up to her tiny, almost unformed chin.

'You'd make a good mum,' Jenny said. 'You seem to know what you're doing.' She watched as Chrissy settled in again.

I suddenly remembered the present, and brought out the

bear for her. Jenny thanked me quietly, tucking it into the bed. There was a knock at the door, and Russell appeared with a bouquet of flowers. I stood up, grinned at him, and stepped over to give him a hug. His eyes were enlarged, and glittering with what I took to be happiness. 'Congratulations,' I said to him. He looked anxiously over at Jen, and I felt my importance slip away. I grew awkwardly conscious that he had more right to time alone with Jen than I did. I kissed Jenny on the forehead, and let her wan half-smile reassure me as I left.

It was the second to last time I saw her.

When Jenny came up to my house a week later, I was deeply asleep. It had taken me a long time to doze off. There were strong winds that night, and the windows and doors rattled intermittently, rousing me every now and then just as I'd managed to sink a little more. I finally settled—and so deeply that the knock entered my mind like an axe. It felt as if I had been separated into two states, the conscious and unconscious moments flailing to find one another again like the two halves of an injured beetle severed by a sharpened spade. I had been in a warm, lulling dream which brimmed slowly with sensations; I saw sunshine on lush grass, a cleared circle in the middle of trees, and a light shaft catching two long-legged, dancing dragonflies: spinning, miniature aerialists. My focus had moved right up to the filigree on one of the transparent wings when, like a stone splintering glass, a fist rapped against my window pane.

After I'd visited Jenny and Chrissy at the ward, I'd promised myself that I would go to see them as soon as they returned home. I'd wanted to visit much earlier, but as I was walking down the corridor from Jenny's room, a senior midwife who had seen me through the glass panel that sectioned off the staff room, stopped me and asked after Jenny. She told me Jenny had told her about me, and had been talking constantly about me coming. 'You're obviously very close to her,' she said. I glowed, said Jenny seemed all right, but tired. The midwife frowned, then she suggested that I leave another visit for a while. I didn't understand.

'She's very drained, and also, as you probably noticed, very depressed.' Her voice dropped, professionally solicitous and soothing. 'It happens to some new mothers. And, as you also probably know, there have been recent family difficulties.'

It was like seeing the shape of a stranger move towards me in an unlit room. Fear drummed in my ears, and I wanted to turn and run—go right back to the cubicle and push in on Jenny and Russell. The tears I had wanted blunderingly to assume meant relief and simple exhaustion were something other . . . but the midwife was insistent: 'She needs rest.' She told me to wait until Jenny was home at the end of the week.

I was woken on the eve of Jenny's scheduled discharge from hospital. Even as I tripped and staggered to the window, I didn't feel any need for caution. I already knew that it would be her. For the past few days, the ward had refused to put me through when I called, although they had let me know when Jenny would be going home. I was certain by then that there was something seriously wrong. I trusted her to get hold of me somehow.

I opened the window, and with a new, wincing awkwardness, Jenny swung herself up to a sitting position on its ledge and slid in. She shrugged off a small backpack and I went back to sit on the edge of my bed, my reactions still muffled by sleep. Jenny quickly trailed me. Her face was alert in a way I had never seen before, though I noticed that the areas under her eyes were a strange shade against her pallor and freckles: as if a blue juice had seeped in under the skin. She held up a hand to my mouth and, at the same time, a finger to her own lips, although we hadn't exchanged a word. We stayed motionless for several seconds, and in the moonlight that washed the room through the partly opened curtains, her widened eyes signalled for me to listen. The house was still, apart from an electric hum which came from the corridor—a slightly faulty light or the refrigerator labouring on in the dark.

Something in Jenny's look frightened me, and I tried to move my head, so that her hand would fall free. She quickly moved her body in closer, and clamped her hand down harder over my mouth. The soft skin on the inside of my lips was forced up hard against my teeth, the sensation moving in pinpricks to my tearducts: the kind of pain that breeds a flashed, sniping response. I tried to bite at her hand, as indignation bristled in me—what did she think she was doing, barging in and treating me like this without a single spoken reassurance?

Jenny's face relaxed a little when I fought to bite out at her hand. Although she kept her palm there for a moment, she released the pressure, and gave a small gesture of apology with her shoulders and elbows. Then she took her hand away, slowly, palm still held towards me, like a gentle fending or to reassure herself of the safety of something precariously balanced.

'I'm sorry, Marie. I'm sorry.' She whispered, almost mouthed, the words.

We sat looking at each other a little longer. Her pupils were enormous in the moonlight: an animal's night vision. I suddenly needed to hug her, and I buried my face in her hair. It smelt of the city air, and was cold, as if she'd been outside for hours. I drew away, and waited. She looked at her hands, which now lay in her lap. I let my eyes focus there as well, an arm around her, and she sat so motionless that it wasn't until I saw a pair of droplets run onto her knuckles that I realised she was crying. That was when my cautious anticipation metamorphosed to real dread.

'It's Chrissy,' she whispered, and a shudder moved through her that I felt all along the side of my body. It was some time before she could control the small aftershocks. To keep back the sobs, she held her breath for several seconds. Then she carried on.

'Dad and Marion—it was all lies about me being able to go home. I should have known, but then I thought I'd be able to leave eventually, like you said . . .' She sounded accusing. 'I've been in a fucking dream world. They've made me sign adoption papers, Marie.' She looked up at me. But my face had numbed. I couldn't make any gesture.

'They bullied and bullied me, they fucking blackmailed me, Dad saying it was for the best, I was really still far too young, I have so much "going" for me'—she wrenched the word—'that I don't want to miss chances, that other people, people who can't have children, would give Chrissy a more stable life. I said no, then they threatened they'd not be able to help me with money at all, that I'd have to learn responsibility and do it all on my own—either that, or face up to my "mistake" and be *sensible*—like I'm still a fucking child!—and give her up for adoption. But, it wasn't even that so much.' She took a swift breath, and let it out again. 'I mean, perhaps I could have kept her still, somehow moved in with Russell straight away—but Marie . . .'

She looked at me in a way that said she was afraid I would reject her, censure her, argue with her. I kept every muscle poised.

'Marie, something went wrong. I didn't expect to feel—something's wrong with the way I feel. And I couldn't fight them any more. I was so tired, and since Chrissy was born, I just didn't know what I wanted any more. I didn't think it would be like that. I thought everything would feel different, better, like there weren't any of the old problems any more. But whenever I looked at her, I just couldn't . . . I mean, I care about her, but I just wanted to look away. It felt like everything was worse, everything was crashing down on me. And then, do you know what that *bitch* did when Dad was out of the room?' All the wired energy sapped from her; she'd talked herself into exhaustion. I wondered then how far she had walked, and in what desperate state. I held onto her more tightly.

'When Dad had gone down the corridor to the Men's, Marion kept on at me about how I couldn't give Chrissy any kind of life. The first time she's talked to me in fucking months, and I get this: I was too young; I was giving up on the education Dad had always wanted for me; Russell and I wouldn't last; look how us kids had screwed up her life; and just when she and Dad were going to be rid of us, I was trying to tie them down. She lit up a cigarette, and was walking closer to me the whole time she was talking, until she came right up to the bed where I was holding Chrissy—and she held the cigarette over Chrissy's head, and then—' Jenny's voice broke from its whisper with a small upwards cry. She smothered her mouth with her hand, the retches as she tried to swallow the sobs taking over her body again. I felt my mind stall, refuse to picture what happened next.

Like Jenny, there was some bedrock part of me that wanted to believe in the goodness of people, that was as persistent as a domesticated, slow-learning laboratory mouse approaching any hand that comes through its cage. Assuming the fingers will just tickle it under the whiskers and offer it titbits of food. Like the mouse nosing forward, we were both stupidly insensible of how ready and instinctive our trust really was.

Jenny told me that Marion lowered the butt of her cigarette quickly and held it to Chrissy's face: so near that Jenny was terrified that the slightest of her movements, even to turn Chrissy free, would brush the baby's cheek against the burning ash. Marion held it there as the length of ash grew, staring Jenny in the face. And a detail that I still can't take in properly or understand all this time later is that Jenny said Marion's eyes welled with tears. Even as she said, with a measure that Jen imitated for me, 'You've got—to sign—those papers. For—your—own—*good*.'

Jenny took my hands, and the skin pinched. 'What if I turned into that, Marie? What if I became like her? She never deserved all her little babies. She didn't deserve them.'

My hands stayed passive within her grip. I had no idea how to respond to her, no idea what to do, nor even where to look.

Then it was as if her account had firmed up some decision for her. She became urgently practical, though tears raced free as she stood and began rummaging in her backpack. I stood up as well, feeling inadequate, superfluous.

'Marie, you have to listen to me, and you can't argue, you can't say anything. Please, please don't say anything. Just help me.' She pulled a pair of long, thin-handled hairdressing scissors from her bag and dumped them on my bed; then she took out a small cardboard carton, and started to take off her clothes. Her breasts, still full and swollen, swung a little, weighing heavily in her light bra.

'I need to borrow something to wear. Something your Mum wouldn't miss. And you're going to have to cut my hair and help me dye it in here. You'll need to go out and get a bucket and some water for me, and something to wrap up the gloves and so on once we've finished.'

I shook my head. 'What—why?'

She stepped close to me, her hands on my shoulders, her eyes focused on mine.

'Marie, I'm never going back there. Never. I can't stay in this place. You know I can't. It's all decided. I'm going to Wellington, and then I'm really going to get out of here.'

Water leapt into my eyes like angry, stabbing questions. She shook her head as if to say I had no right to cry.

'I can't even bear to be on the same piece of dirt as those *fuckers*. I'm going to leave for Melbourne. Russell thinks he can get work there—he knows friends who can set him up. And I'll look for work too.'

I remembered Russell's joke about his savings and honeymoon airfares. Jenny tightened her grip on my shoulder, and it hurt.

But not as much as the way she seemed to have forgotten that she was leaving me behind as well. I pushed her hand away.

'But why Melbourne? It's so far—why can't you just move up north? I'll be there when term starts. We can be together. I mean, you can't just leave. You can't. I bet you don't even have a passport. Have you thought about that? And what if Russell leaves you while you're over there? What if you can't find a job?'

She looked at me with an unexpected, unrestrained hatred. 'And what if I stay here, Marie? What then? Chrissy's adoptive parents live somewhere up north, but they don't want me to have contact till she's old enough to choose for herself. What about thinking I might see them? Knowing I wasn't strong enough to keep her? What's left for me here?'

I tried to understand her solution, but walked backwards and dropped onto my bed again, finally letting myself weep properly. 'There's me.'

Even in that closed room, it felt like the words were being torn away and drowned in the wind that clattered against the window. I felt hope whip away from me, a thin silk kite shredded on a tree branch then yanked away over the rooftops.

Jenny came to sit with me, and buried her head against my shoulder. 'I wish you could come with me. But Marie, I'm going to call you. I'll phone as soon as I get to Wellington, to let you know that I'm okay, and then I'll call from Melbourne. You're the only one I care about in this place now.'

'What about Chrissy? You could say no. You could say they forced you . . .'

She shook her head. I had no right to ask, or to feel: her life was already bisected from mine.

'I don't know how I feel about Chrissy.' There was a strained silence. 'Something's not there. And I can't look after her like that. I'm frightened. I can't do it. I don't know how to do it. What if I tried to hurt her one day? I really am doing this for her, don't you understand?'

There was something else. I could tell from the way her hand moved over her face and her hair that she was unsure whether to tell me. I stared at her until she met my eyes. A dark sail of doubt drew its shadow across her. 'Marie,' she said, her voice cooled under its quick wing. 'I've used one of Dad's cards. I know his PIN number. I saved the printout that came with it, months ago. I got it out of his rubbish bin. I wasn't really sure why I did it at the time—just something to keep from them, I guess. And I've taken the week's grocery money from Marion's wallet. I know they'll try to find me.'

Oh, Christ, the money seemed pitiful to me, faced with her departure. I tried to make her see it.

'Gerald will look for you anyway, Jen. He'll be worried sick. What the hell am I going to tell him?'

She didn't want to hear this, to feel that her plans could be crumpled up and tossed aside like a poor sketch. Yet her guess that Gerald would try to find her had made her go to these extremes.

'Marie, you've got to help me.'

I felt so ill I had to close my eyes. Everything in the room seemed to have lost its defining outline; Jenny's face, and all the objects around us, were refracted by an uneasy light, as if they were on the point of changing state, and the walls seemed to draw away from me, leaving me as a point small and distant, removed from them. I couldn't ground myself in anything, couldn't focus and test the reality of what she was saying against the solidity of our surroundings. I tried to understand—I knew why she was going. But I couldn't imagine the loss. And the picture of Chrissy, her face screwed up and concentrating so hard on the business of living, even as she slept, kept drawing me back to incomprehension.

Yet I also remembered that afternoon long ago when I had witnessed one of Marion's assaults, when she hit Jenny with the dog leash for having cigarettes. Then I thought of Marion smoking. Marion with a cigarette butt, coming closer. And Jenny, not reaching out to touch Chrissy when I held her close. I rubbed my eyes until sharp, pointed lights replaced those scenes.

Jenny went to sit in front of my mirror, where she carefully but quickly snipped at her fringe with the scissors. Then she took great clumps of her hair between the blades. It shrank and shrank, until it formed a soft red cloud that hovered just beneath her ears. She looked older—or was it younger? The effect was so alien that I couldn't decide. All the angles of her face seemed to have altered. Without looking around, she passed the scissors over her shoulder, and asked me to even up the back. I responded, not knowing why I did. My hands shook, and I took the edges up a little higher than I meant to, exposing one or two dark moles that had previously been hidden. Her neck looked so pale, like the albino root of a grass blade.

The contrast between the tones of her skin and hair was exaggerated even more when she finished dyeing the bob. We had to wait for so long for the dye to set that I was sure someone would wake and discover us before it was ready. Then we were left with towels and plastic gloves that were darkly stained: black cherry, the colour was called. I'd have to get rid of them somehow. I couldn't stop staring at Jenny as she tidied up around the room, repacking her bag before risking a visit to the bathroom.

When she came back, she asked me again to select some old clothes. There were plenty that I hadn't discarded yet, although they were too small for me and I was meant to do a final cleanout before I left at the end of the summer. Something in me reacted to Jenny's uncharacteristic urgency. She was working so rapidly now, so desperately, that I had an automatic impulse to do the same: just to follow, as in a crisis, unthinking, responding with the unnatural calm of an emergency, the way I would have left a burning building at her word.

I pulled out a neatly waisted cotton dress printed with moss-green leaves, and to go with it, a jade-green cardigan with deep-plum buttons. The dress looked like a vintage 1940s party dress on Jenny; on me, it always looked like a little girl's school frock. She folded up the black denim mini skirt she'd been wearing, which had extra panels that she'd sewn in around the waistband. It was the same one she had worn the night she met Russell.

As she dressed, the panic that had been partially suspended by helping in her transformation came back.

'Jenny, you have to phone me, like you said. You will, won't you? You'll keep me absolutely, to the last minute, up to date on what you decide to do? Do you promise?'

'I promise,' she whispered.

She asked me if I would help her with her make-up. It was all new—not the shades she usually wore. I recognised the brand as the only one that was sold at the hospital store; I'd visited there several times when I'd gone to meet Mum at the end of her nursing shifts: it was where people could buy cards, chocolate, flowers and other small gifts, if they had arrived empty handed. It made me ask whether the hospital knew she had gone, and she said yes, they had discharged her twelve hours early, after Chrissy had been taken away.

I stared at the cosmetics, knowing I was going to help her, just because she was Jenny, my friend, not because I understood.

I crouched down before her, lightly touching all the sticks, brushes and pads to her face: foundation, kohl, eyebrow pencil, mascara, lip outliner, lipstick, blush. We had done this for each other so many times, experimenting in our rooms, and there was that occasion, during a school play season, when I had deepened her frown and laughter lines with a fine pencil: aging her in the way that would resonate with me unexpectedly all those years afterwards, in the middle of a crowded, rush-hour train. I felt as if I were hurting her and didn't know how to stop.

I had to stand back to check over what I'd done. Alongside the dramatic transformation of Jenny's hair, my efforts with make-up seemed slight. But the subtlety was right: heavy lines and richer colours would have called unnatural attention to her. And it was enough. I wouldn't have recognised Jenny if I'd glimpsed her in the street unexpectedly. Nobody would have.

Now, the sweet, cakey scent of make-up foundation always brings back a sharp sting of anxiety, and I see Jenny, her pupils enlarged, her hands shaking a little as she pauses to think between movements: the signs of a wild spirit that thinks it's trapped; the signals that meant she believed that if she didn't run now, she never would. As if the rest of her life had some deadline.

Crumpling her tissue, Jenny ran over her plans for me one last time. Outside, birds had begun to clamour. The approaching sun had stirred the night sky with the slightest touch of blue. It filtered between the gaps in my curtains, touched everything in the room, and gave all the objects a new fullness and depth. It filled the tired hollows in Jenny's cheeks and the lines alongside her mouth with a softening shadow. I had never seen the world at this hour; it felt as if the new tone entered and changed everything.

Lightly giddy with lack of sleep, suddenly I wanted to leave as well—leave with Jenny. I could feel how simple, how utterly, devastatingly easy it would be to pack a bag, take some money, look around the room and go. But Jenny was whispering, fiercely collected. She was going to dump the clothes she'd been wearing when she left home in an alleyway nearby, half way between her house and mine. I was to tell no one—*no one*—that I had seen her.

'This is it,' she said, and something like desire and despair gripped in her with a dangerous fusion, so that her face was shot through with a disturbing ecstasy. 'I'm doing it.'

She assured me that every logistical detail I could possibly worry about had been seen to: she had her own passport from when she'd holidayed in Australia with her family when she was thirteen, the summer before I met her. She said that she had enough money, she'd taken out all her university savings. She knew where she was meeting Russell, and she was catching the 5 a.m. bus to Nelson that morning—the first service. I fumbled in my bag for extra money. I forced her to take everything—the last fortnight's pay packet from my job at Dad's supermarket. I wasn't convinced about her financial situation, though she said Russell had also given her the money to get to Wellington. From Nelson, she would get another bus to Picton, then from Picton the ferry to the North Island, and then, in Wellington, a taxi to where Russell was staying. She hoped she would be there some time after midnight, a little under twenty-four hours away. There was nothing else I could think of. Russell had already bought the plane tickets; she told me he had gone up to Wellington two days ago and found reduced fares, so a large part of his—small—savings were left. He'd sent the ticket to her by post, as she'd requested, just in case she was late getting to him or the airport for any reason. There was nothing wrong with what she was doing, she told me. She had to do it. Get away. Now or never.

And then she was gone. One last embrace. The dawn contracted: became arid and blank. Even the mark her lipstick left on my cheek could have been the red of skin pressed up against my own arm during the span of a deep sleep. Not a trace was left to give her away.

Jenny didn't phone me the next day—or the next. I knew they were planning to leave for Melbourne late that evening so I was surprised she'd forgotten to call. That was what we'd arranged. I clung on to her promise.

When four days mounted up, the hours accumulating inside me like a scream, I began to get frightened. Jenny had promised. I had made her promise so that I would know she was safe. She couldn't forget.

On the fifth day, Gerald phoned. I was frantic when I realised it wasn't Jen, but I carried out our plan—which was to tell him that we'd talked on the phone, but I hadn't seen her since she'd been in hospital. I also took the opportunity to say things I'd always thought I couldn't say to someone's parents. I said that if Jenny wasn't with them, it was no surprise to me: 'You've driven her out.' Gerald hung up abruptly.

I was left with even more questions. How could anybody force an adoption on someone else? Had Jenny given in too easily? My mother had told me, after my visit to the hospital, that the depression women could get after giving birth didn't have to last. They could end up loving their babies just the same.

That night, on the radio, a description of Jenny was released—and it was there too in the evening edition of the paper. The vagueness enraged me, as did the report. It said that the family were terribly worried, because Jenny had recently 'decided' to adopt out her child and 'may have been distressed'.

The next morning, some women's clothes were found by the coastline, in a cove that it was possible to get to only at low tide. They weren't the clothes Jenny's father described her leaving the house in—and they weren't the clothes she told me that she was going to leave in an alleyway near her house: nothing was discovered there. Jammed into a hollow, soaked, with Jenny's bag, they were mine: the dress and cardigan that Jen had borrowed. Her bag held a diary. When the pages dried out, some of Jen's song lyrics were legible, along with a few entries, the most recent of which told the story of Marion's threats, and Jenny's plans. Nothing about these differed from what she had told me. 'I'm doing it,' she'd written. 'Finally getting out of here. Just wish I could get her voice out of my head as well. Wish I could stop all the memories of here.' The bag also contained the cosmetics and a few changes of light clothing. Her passport wasn't there—and apart from some loose coins, nothing like the amount of money she'd told me she had.

The police knew that Russell was in Wellington but were able to confirm that he had been there for some days before her disappearance, waiting for her, and he was quickly dismissed from their inquiries. Desperate with worry, he had in the end phoned the police himself to report her missing, not knowing that the same day Marion and Gerald contacted the police in the South Island.

When the police came to me, then took me to the station to show me the evidence, I couldn't do it—I couldn't carry on. I no longer knew if I'd done the right thing: I was so frightened. I told them the clothes were mine, but that Jenny had borrowed them and had been planning to leave. I told them that she had asked me not to tell; I told them how we had cut and coloured her hair. I asked to be allowed to look through her wardrobe to see if anything else was missing. They patted me on the back, gave me tissues and sweet tea, told me that what I said confirmed what they'd read in her diary, and that they knew Jenny had been unhappy at home. And from the way they spoke of Marion, it seemed they were only formally civil to her.

The police escorted me to Jenny's house, where I looked through her belongings. Jonathon was there. He followed us to Jen's bedroom, and watched me silently from the doorway. I told them that something was missing: her favourite Indian skirt; the blue one with silver bells and silver thread. And a white-sleeved blouse, which had tiny clover shapes cut from the fabric for coolness. I elaborated more on the press description—told them Jenny had tan moles on the back of her neck and behind her ears. That she had small chickenpox scars on her forehead, a birthmark over her collarbone, and three pale pink scars cut in parallel on her left forearm. They looked at Jonathon, and he nodded. He didn't touch me as we walked out—just turned away.

The police transcribed my statement, and next to a more detailed description in the paper and on the TV news, they finally showed photos of Jenny that were taken over the past year. One of them focused closely on her smile. It was a detail from the shot taken of us together on the night we'd lied about the senior dance.

Russell called me soon after the new description was released. He'd returned from Wellington to wait for news. He told me Jenny had phoned him from a call booth on the night I saw her, some time after leaving me, just to let him know she was okay. 'Be strong,' she'd said, and 'I'll be all right.'

The conversation with Russell was awful. He sounded so removed, his voice erased at the edges, scattering like particles into the telephone static. As I asked more and more questions, I knew I was pushing him farther and farther away. But I knew it would be the only chance I'd have to ask. It was like trying to paint a hurried picture before the light withdrew from a landscape. The vagueness of Jenny's father's description of her just after she disappeared made me feel that, if more time went by, people's recollections would become weaker and weaker: her voice, her gestures losing colour until there was only the diluted, hazy blue of distance. Russell was confused, disoriented: sentences would spark up again from the silence as if I were losing and regaining a signal on a radio band.

'If she did it herself,' he said, 'why didn't I see . . .'

I couldn't stop myself from interrupting. 'Why would she have gone to all the trouble of coming here and changing her clothes if she was planning that?'

I thought I had lost him—I imagined him putting down the receiver on a side table somewhere, walking from the room, door swinging slowly like a metronome behind him. But he spoke again. 'Why would she leave if we'd already organised . . . ? There must have been someone else involved. Someone who saw her out on the coast road that morning . . . who took her money . . .'

In a moment of nauseating clarity, I pictured a beaten-up car parked along a coastline and a silhouetted form moving towards Jenny. Russell and I sat at the end of each other's silences, waiting. I groped for other possibilities. Wondered if Jenny could have had an alternative plan, set aside from all that she had told me.

There was no way of knowing.

Russell, voice dwindling, said, 'Marie, I'll call you back.'

He didn't, for days. So I tried to find him—going to his old work, trying his former number—but he wasn't there. Initially, I was desperate at the idea of losing contact. I wanted to see him, to be with someone who loved Jenny, who understood what it was like to be thinking only of her, to be talking to her inside their head every step of each day. But the more I re-ran our phone call, the more I realised that even in that fractured conversation we had been driven back into our separate losses. It was as if we had been talking about different Jennys. The one I was left with was the one who walked and moved within me, whether I woke or slept.

So Russell went, too. I don't know how soon he left town again—at least, I assume he left: there was nothing to keep him there any longer: no job, no Jenny, and then there was his unused ticket to Melbourne. Just like Catherine and Blake: first he was there, and then he wasn't. There was once, though, when I wondered . . . much later, when I was at a gig, at university up north. A few bands were playing—and there, as I arrived late, I saw someone in profile. Tall, although with dark hair, he moved through the crowd in the opposite direction, carrying a blue guitar case and touching people on the shoulder now and then, asking them to let him pass. It was like a leap back to the night we had met. I stared, tried to push my way through the crowd, back the way I had come, tracking his profile, waiting for the hot gulp of recognition to hit me again. But when we had both pushed through to the foyer and he met my eyes, his glance registered nothing. I dropped back, unsure then, and watched him run down the stairs and swing out to the footpath.

Just a few weeks after that call from Russell, I should have left for university. But it felt as if my life had been suspended. I was worried that if I left town, I might miss news of Jenny. I managed to postpone some of my course enrolment until midway through the academic year, but would have to pick up the majority of my papers in the following cycle. For months the authorities gave no reports of having traced Jenny's passport. Then, one afternoon, my mother and father took me into the living room, and sat me down. They had received another visit from the police while I was out wandering the beach.

They told me to accept that Jenny was dead. The police said that it would be on the news that night: the case was to be held over indefinitely. Although they had no way of confirming whether it was accidental, suicidal or involved an assailant, their suspicions remained that Jenny had drowned. They had taken divers along the coast. Jonathon had turned up with his scuba suit and had fought to be let on to the police boat. They did eventually allow him aboard, but physically restrained him from going under with the police team.

My father held my hand, and told me that surely the sea would return her body to us. He tried to say it gently; said that then we could feel at rest, that our demonic doubts could be exorcised. But then he added, 'The way that shoreline gets battered with those waves . . .' and I began to cry. My mother took my face in her palms, then pulled me against her chest, and said, 'Oh, Marie, we're so, so sorry.' Her voice broke, but I still heard the rest. She added, 'Thank God it wasn't you.' I shoved myself roughly away from them both. All the directionless feelings of vengeance and fury that I had stored up behind my bedroom door for the past two months, staring painfully dry-eyed at the ceiling, as if it might crack open like sealed lips and speak some answer, suddenly erupted.

'You selfish, selfish fucking *bastards!*' I kicked over the coffee table, then kicked it again. By then they were both standing, paralysed. 'You say to accept that my *best friend* is dead! And then you say, *Thank God!* You can go to hell. You can go to hell, go to hell, go to hell with whoever, *whoever* did this!' I walked out of the room and slammed the door, willing the whole house to collapse around their ears from the reverberations. Some glass in the living room crashed from a shelf. It was a derisive sound. I cried in my room until my whole body was parched.

I remember nearly everything about the first weeks following that afternoon. As much as I loathed the world for saying I had to accept that Jenny was dead, my parents' quiet words had released some force. Ever since the police had found Jenny's clothes—my clothes—I had guessed, deep down. But hearing it from my father made it more real.

It is as if a particular state of shock doesn't numb us, but instead makes everything unbearably clear. I even remember the first morning, waking up thinking: now I am without her.

I was aware of a grainy sensation under my eyelids as I crept closer to full consciousness. My whole body hurt, and I folded my limbs up to form a shield against the beam of daylight which prodded at me like a sharp stick. I know I wondered how the human body could keep on going like this. How could I keep on breathing, breathing, when reality had changed so? I felt my heartbeat pulse at my neck and high under my ribs where they met in the tip of a pointed arc, as if Jenny's disappearance had somehow thrown all the involuntary actions of my body into relief. Death had come so close to this house, this room, that it seemed palpable, its charged, hovering electrodes sparking silently, invisibly, above me, about to descend and send their massive voltage through every nerve filament, every synapse...

A strong image of Jenny's profile, her eyes creased in laughter, her head tilting back, shot up before my vision, and I tried to hold it, moving my gaze over all the familiar details as if this were my last chance to confirm the reality of her. I remembered the time we had talked about her real mother, and like the temporary brilliancies sent out by a skyrocket all the colours dissipated. I rolled over as each sob winded me with a steel-capped kick.

One thing in particular from those first weeks after Jenny's clothes were found by the beach still has the power to unseat me. To make me want to shake myself into some simple, domestic activity that will centre me again: boil a kettle, stack magazines, finger along the slender variegated leaves of a spider plant, test the soil and see if it needs water . . .

It was one Saturday afternoon. My parents had gone out visiting, to meet up with my sisters, but they had quietly, carefully, left me alone, guessing that I would say no to the invitation. Or perhaps they had never intended to ask me; had decided that I needed the house to myself for a while. I knew that whenever we were in the same room, they were watching me as attentively as if I were surfacing from a long illness.

I was reading a newspaper, scanning it with a frown, disbelieving, as always, that there could be no new report that gave an answer to my waiting. I had little real hope any more—but as my father had said, any solid evidence would let me get on with truly absorbing just what it was like to live without it. A noise from the street made me look up and move to the window. It was the hollow clop of horses' hooves: a bizarre sound for the small street we lived in. Still I waited for mounted riders to pass by, expecting to see them in helmets, the rolling movement in their bodies following the forward motion of the animals. Two horses did glide across my vision, necks bowing and rising in a trained synchrony, their heads crowned with giant black plumes that waved, backwards and forwards, to the metre of the horses' slow trot. They were drawing a carriage; its driver, who wore top hat and tails, sat erect and still, and held the whip at his side to a militant attention. The black carriage was iced with an enormous display of white flowers. I could see through the windows of its cab: a small coffin rode within it, alone. Trailing after the horses came low, sleek vehicles, the kind I imagined were owned by collectors. Each car had its own cape of flowers draped over its roof. The people inside had their heads bowed;

one sat slumped against the doors. A build-up of traffic, also unusual for our street, slowed behind them, and then the whole train passed by. I stood in the room's silence, waiting to define exactly what had taken me from my seat.

I stayed motionless by the window. It was as if a sliver of time had dislodged from another century, another country, and worked itself under the day's thin, transparent surface; the dark funeral a foreign splinter, bringing with it an ache that was at once unexpectedly fresh and yet too familiar. As a scaffolding lorry and then a van painted with plumbers' phone numbers carried on through the street to a new house site a little further down, I had to ask myself if the cortège had really existed. I had never seen anything like it before.

Disorienting, trance-like, those moments echoed the nightmares which had begun after the police found Jenny's clothes. I would half wake, with a terrible pain in my head and, finding myself unable to see, try to stumble across to the light switch or to my parents' room. I would then find I hadn't moved from my original waking position, and would again be aware of the pain, again try to roll myself out of bed and get help . . . and so it would go on, in ever-intensifying levels of fear, until I lurched truly awake and realised it was all right, there was no pain, I could see, I could move.

That is what dying must be like, I thought.

I woke so shaken that soon I was afraid to sleep, convinced these nightmares would re-surface.

This spiral of waking sleep had left me even more unsure of what was real and what was only my mind revolving over and over the cryptic fact of Jenny's silence. Was this *real*? Was it true that Jenny would never come back, not ever? Hadn't she just gone away, like she'd said? I found myself looking up from a book to gaze out the window, waiting for her to walk past and turn down the front path; or I would will her, *will her* to surprise me by working free the rusty old lock on the side gate and come round the back to find me sitting in the garden.

The potency of this daytime wishing gradually subsided. Yet at night, the dreams continued. And they began to concern Jenny herself. I still have them sometimes, though any number of months may lapse between them.

They always start in the park. We are spinning on the merry-go-round, or racing higher on the swings, trying to be first to touch an overhanging tree with the tips of our toes. We are drunk, our heads tipped back, necks exposed to the cold blades of star and moonlight: red wine leaks from the sides of our mouths, although we're trying not to let it spill as we laugh at some story. Then, at a shift in the wind, the mood alters. In slow motion, Jenny rises and walks to the edge of the park, where the darkness redoubles. I call and call but the whiteness of her arms and legs dissolves into the night like snow melting on black asphalt.

I run to the park's perimeter, and see the beginnings of water: a pond that swells into a lake, a lake that swells into an ocean. Waves lap at the grass, the two greens blurred as they meet, like a land-bound horizon line. I see Jenny again, wading in naked, stirring sparks of phosphorescence over the water's surface. Her clothes are limp on the grass, like balloons sucked of air.

I sense a dark oval to the left of my vision that scuds away as I call after the moonlit form that walks farther into the water. The shadow that races from the frame of my dream suggests the height of a man. Yet sometimes—it feels so very close. As if it may have been I who cast it, had I walked beneath a direct source of light—my shadow coming up from behind, engulfing me for a moment, then racing on, straining to leap from my shoulders. I turn, try to catch some movement to verify what it was that has thrown the shape, see nothing, turn back, and Jenny has gone. A last flash of red hair, floating like weed with the rise of a wave—and then nothing.

I plunge in. Dive, weave lower, searching, eyes stinging with salt and bitter sand. Deeper down, my lungs now stretched like fabric on a frame, I see her. Her eyes are closed, her lips shut in the secretive smile of the dead. Thousands of minuscule bubbles, glistening, cling to her skin, where they tremble. Some break free, as if the exertion of holding her down has become too great. As I kick towards her, slowly her skin begins to give off a green luminescence. Her form begins to stream from her, her body soluble in the ocean. Like water added and added to a painted shape on rice paper, the colours bleed from her. Small copper and blue fish flit into the space she has occupied, mouthing at the coral-like bones left behind. I open my mouth to call, and icy fluid pours in.

The police let me have Jenny's diary after they had removed the filled-in pages for evidence. I wrote to her—

> Come back.
> Why don't you call me?
> Come back.

Now, when I think of where we lived, I think of grey pebbles, grey ocean, the yellowed froth of boiling surf in a storm—and a wet, cotton-print dress stuffed into a split in grey rock. When people here ask me, 'What's it like in New Zealand?' I know there is a much broader picture. That I should talk about the coincidences and connections that bond people together. Bring in the lush bush, the subtropical rainforests, the mud pools, mountains and tussock-land, tribal history, what it's like to come from a small town there. But in my mind, I keep returning to that one beach.

For years, this has been my buried story. No body was ever found, and neither was a passport with Jenny's name registered at any international Customs. While I tried to say that my friend had died, I was left with those two puzzles. They have shaped me as much as the loss.

I did come to, as the lessening of grief seems to be: slipping into a different state of consciousness. But the grief is always there. It's like water that has slowly seeped into soil: invisible, yet still running the concealed root network, the subterranean life.

And I did go on to university, determinedly refusing my father's last offer of work, and majoring in sociology, where I made several adequate but never very fully meant friendships. It strikes me now that this may have been because of a new inability to trust. Being too broken to rely on anyone as fully as I had before.

All the time at university, however, restlessness opened in me like a vivid flower, until I finally left the country, heaping all the vague dissatisfaction I felt at twenty-two on to 'this place', thinking that it was my background I had to cast off instead of realising that I needed to examine my own faults, and echoing, I can see now, Jenny's words, all those years before. I wanted to travel, but didn't really know why any more. Perhaps for just that easy fix of thinking I was 'getting somewhere'. Or perhaps, because my life had been cleaved from its course when Jenny died, the only way to react to the cruelty of change was to change, and change, and change again. Trying to beat chance. Trying not to expect, to plan, to place faith, to build: using the newness of each location as an excuse for never feeling settled.

Eventually, I used up that restlessness, too. I scrutinised the past a little less often. It became like a photo that I knew too well—that left out too much of what went on beyond its outline. Then I met Joss in London. After many months—in fact, almost a year—of his loyalty and persistence, I was still insisting that I didn't think I was ready for more than a friendship; and then he said he was considering a move to Edinburgh. I crumpled. I begged him to stay. Then I begged him to let me go as well. I said if he wouldn't let me, I'd follow him anyway. And he started to shake. He said he was a fake, a fraud; saying that he was going to leave had been his last resort, a last attempt to get through to me. I finally stepped right off the edge and into love. Gradually, if I can reduce it to such simplistic terms, I found a renewed focus, even a sense of ambition. As if confidence and finally having someone else to confide in had coalesced.

I never forgot Jenny. That much is evident from the dreams that continue to visit me. And I still consider her the closest friend I've ever had. That this has remained so is perhaps one of the reasons why her disappearance haunts me. Once I met Joss, I realised that the intensity of my high-school friendship could only be matched by another kind of love. It had been a preparation, a partnership. JennyandMarie.

Yet why, if the dreams do come less often now, did today's sighting so affect me? I know Joss must have gone to bed unsure of why I was so unnerved. 'But can't you see?' I whisper to the walls. 'My memories of her make me. Can't you see that losing her when I did, in the way that I did, both changed and set everything?' There was no natural end to our friendship. We didn't outgrow each other.

She was there at so many of my firsts—is that what it is? When I try to share in the school anecdotes that people tell, and I start with 'My friend Jenny and I . . .', their faces never seem to register the *firstness* of it all. I want their reactions to give me some access back into those feelings: the thrill of innocence on the verge of breaking open, trembling, like a young girl's hands on any first night. Nearly all my memories of growing up must include her, and so nearly all my memories must include her loss.

So what if, having been through the stations of grief, and their slow, repeated passage over the years, what if what you've tried to teach yourself to accept all this time as a death becomes altered? What if the person comes back?

The boundaries have shifted. The person cannot be who you thought. They have run you through with the deepest of psychic suffering. They have taken their fraudulent leave from you as if you were no more than a place, a wayside tavern at which they've supped and rested, and upon which they've closed the door and forgotten.

Or have they? Has she? Did Jenny die? Or did she disappear?

The questions won't cease. Yet I also know that even the answers are not uncomplicated. It would be another beginning, another looping spiral of questions. Perhaps it is the nature of the question that troubles me more. What does it mean if someone disappears, if someone dies? Is it different?

Thinking I have seen Jenny—I tear the nib of my pen through several layers of the stationery pad I still have on my knees for the letter to my parents—doesn't answer any of my questions. It only repeats them again after all these years, and feeds hope that she has survived, hope that she has succeeded. Hope: that thin, ragged boy in a cage, holding out an even thinner bone through the bars, and piercing my memory with it.

Thinking that I've seen her has also told me that I am still carrying a small part of Jenny's dilemma. It's left lodged in me the way a cord that's tied too tightly around the stem of a young sapling will be taken into the flesh, so that the tree grows deformed, trunk swollen and bulging around the throttling string.

Chrissy became the wrong kind of anchor for Jenny. While part of me says, How can I have children before I know who their mother will be, before I know I've tried my best to become who I want to be?, there is also that memory of the sudden, overwhelming *irruption* of love that I felt for Chrissy.

Did Jenny do the right thing? Have I?

I hear someone come in through the main doorway of our rickety building and up the stairs to one of the other flats. I remember talking to one of the tenants over a drink in our shared garden when he'd first moved in. He, a Venezuelan, told me that leaving his country was like 'a little death. A good death. A cut, but that has healed, and no scar. My rebirth,' he said. 'The past behind me, and I can start again, but with experience.' I was intrigued, because my own feelings are so different. I may have travelled initially for adventure, to live out all those teenage dreams of escape that Jenny and I had; perhaps making that 'cut' was what I thought I was doing at the time, shaking off my small-town self, thinking I could become someone other, someone better. But there was never any 'cut'. Instead, there are cuttings: hundreds of scenes and memories that I carry with me, that have taken permanent root and put out their light-hungry tendrils into the present. As these uncurl all over again, I wonder, are the stories I've always told Joss enough? For the first time since I left, I can admit that one day I might be ready for more. Ready to show Joss the people and places from my past, ready to go back with him, to look, and consider.

It's late: half-past three. Still not tired, I go to the window and gaze from our second-floor flat to the street below. Most of the terraced houses are dark, but one or two lights burn. The night buses seemed to have stopped, but a black cab runs down the street and pulls up to let out two men. One drops his keys, and the other teeters a bit. They manage to work the three or four locks to the main door of their building, and disappear, arms around each other. Then the street's deserted, a rare moment of stillness in its constant humming. I half watch for the urban fox I've seen near rubbish bins, that vaults low walls, lithe as a cat. It probably lives in the nearby Hackney marshes, where they're threatening to build some new hypermarket. But there's no quiet, loping visitor: not the kind of grace you can seek, it has to come unbidden.

Joss will be dreaming. The thought of him, the daytime lines of his face smoothed in sleep, makes me feel again how precious and fragile any kind of love is.

Yes.

I won't be able to take his advice, and forget the woman I saw today. I will always wonder whether I saw Jenny, and whether or not she is still alive.

But now, as I reexamine all the reasons for why she may have concealed her life from me, that softening of the woman's face as the train pulled away from the station offers me another clue. Perhaps deception, even of me—even of Russell—was needed for Jenny to achieve the perfect escape. Perhaps we dragged her down; perhaps even we would have been too much of a tie to the town and the people she loathed. Yet that small, naked branch of a smile that began after what I think was the frisson of recognition: that tells me something else. If her escape was perfect, her nascent pleasure in recognising me confirms that I helped her to achieve it. And—if it was Jenny—she owes a small portion of her freedom to me.

Wherever she is now, whoever she has become, inside that freedom (and yes, I will say it: even if that freedom is death's liberation) there is still a part of me that is with her—and always will be.